I accept.

The words ran ▮▮▮▮▮▮▮▮▮▮▮▮▮▮▮▮▮▮▮▮ iad emotions to sw▮▮▮

At one time he'd dreamed of being married to Belinda, having children and building a future based on love. Fate had given him a twisted version of them.

Whoever was after Belinda was cunning, and working off some master plan that had its basis in some kind of madness. If what Derek believed was true, that somehow he and Belinda were connected in the mind of somebody who wanted to harm her, then what sort of repercussions would their marriage have?

He sensed approaching danger, felt the vibration of an advancing train. And Derek had the distinct feeling that he and Belinda were chained together on the railroad tracks.

Dear Reader,

Take three sisters, a failing ranch, a bevy of bad guys and three strong, handsome cowboys and you have the ingredients for Cheyenne Nights, my new series for Harlequin Intrigue.

Ranch life in Wyoming takes a special breed of woman. The Connor sisters are that unique breed. They derive their strength from and share a bond with each other and with their land. The only thing missing in each of their lives is love.

Developing three very special men for the Connor sisters was pure joy. They possess all the qualities I hope the readers will love. I know I adore them.

I hope you enjoy the stories of these strong women as they fight for their home, encounter danger and discover the men who will bring them passion and love on those Cheyenne Nights.

Happy reading,

Carla Cassidy

Sunrise Vows
Carla Cassidy

Harlequin Books

TORONTO • NEW YORK • LONDON
AMSTERDAM • PARIS • SYDNEY • HAMBURG
STOCKHOLM • ATHENS • TOKYO • MILAN
MADRID • WARSAW • BUDAPEST • AUCKLAND

ISBN 0-373-22419-2

SUNRISE VOWS

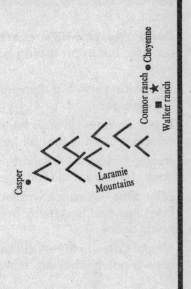

WYOMING

Casper

Laramie
Mountains

Connor ranch • Cheyenne

Walker ranch

CAST OF CHARACTERS

Belinda Connor—Somebody is threatening her life.

Derek Walker—He's returned to protect Belinda, but in protecting her will he destroy her?

Teddy King—A big man—does he harbor a big grudge?

Roger Eaton—He says he wants to find his adopted sister. Is that all he wants?

Janice Kirkwood—Belinda's best friend—but does she have a hidden agenda?

Billy Sims—A ranch worker with a problem. Does he want to destroy Belinda and all she holds dear?

Henry Carsworth—A successful businessman. Is he a potential killer, as well?

Prologue

"Hurry, Colette. You know Abby is waiting for us." Belinda Connor grabbed her younger sister's hand, urging her to run faster.

Overhead a full moon spilled down silvery shards of light, giving the landscape a surreal, otherworldly aura.

In the distance, on a small rise, stood an ancient oak tree, its branches gnarled and misshapen. The dragon tree. And beneath its benevolent foliage Belinda could see their older sister waiting for them.

"Come on, Colette," Belinda said again, tugging her faster. "You know Abby wouldn't have called for this meeting unless it was important."

"I know. I'm hurrying as fast as I can," Colette exclaimed.

By the time they reached the tree, both Belinda and Colette were out of breath. Colette leaned against the trunk of the tree, slivers of moonbeams highlighting her youthful features. Abby sank to sit in the sweet-scented, dewy grass, the moonlight caressing her straight nose and the strong thrust of her jaw.

For a moment as Belinda looked first at her

younger sister then at her older one, love swelled up in her heart. Oh, there were times twelve-year-old Colette could be a real pest, and Abby, at fifteen could be a know-it-all, but they weren't just her sisters, they were her best friends.

"What's going on?" Colette finally caught her breath.

"Yeah, Abby. What's going on? Why'd you call us here?" Belinda asked.

Abby wrapped her arms around her knees and rocked back and forth. "I found some papers today in Mom's dresser drawer."

"What kind of papers?" Belinda asked.

Abby looked first at her, then at Colette. "Adoption papers."

The words hung in the air and echoed hollowly in Belinda's heart. "Adoption papers?" she asked, breaking the silence that followed Abby's statement. "Adoption papers for who?"

"I didn't look. I was looking for Mom's yellow scarf and saw an envelope in her drawer." Abby raked a hand through her short blond hair. "It was just a manila envelope and written on it was 'adoption papers.' I saw it, then heard Mom coming down the hall so I didn't get a chance to open it. I went back in later to look, but the papers weren't there anymore."

Belinda felt the blood leave her face as her heart beat an unsteady rhythm. "But…but that means one of us must be…"

"No," Colette interrupted. "No, I don't want to hear about it, I don't even want to think about it." Colette leaned forward and reached for Abby's hand, then grabbed Belinda's. Belinda squeezed back tightly. "We're sisters. The three of us and no stupid papers will ever change that."

"Belinda? Do you feel the same way about it?" Abby asked.

It's me, a tiny voice whispered inside Belinda's head. *I'm the one who doesn't really belong.* She squeezed both her sisters' hands. "Of course," she answered. "I don't ever want to know which one of us might be in that folder."

Abby stood and reached into her pocket. "I was hoping you guys would say that." She pulled out a large safety pin. "I vote we become blood sisters and we vow we'll never try to find out which one of us might be adopted."

She opened the wicked-looking pin, the sharp point gleaming in the moonlight. Colette and Belinda watched as she pricked her skin. As the blood welled up on her fingertip, she handed the pin to Belinda, who stabbed her own finger.

Colette frowned, her bottom lip caught between her teeth. "Do it for me, Belinda," she said, holding out her finger and squeezing her eyes tightly closed.

Again love welled up in Belinda's heart. Silly Colette, who could face a mountain lion and not be afraid, couldn't stand the sight of blood, especially her own. Belinda pierced her finger with a sharp jab.

"Sisters forever," Abby proclaimed solemnly as she held her finger toward them.

"Sisters forever," Belinda echoed, and pressed her finger against Abby's.

"And no matter what happens, we never read those

stupid papers,'' Colette exclaimed, then added her finger to theirs, forming a triangle of unity.

With the innocence of youth and the optimism of girlhood, they truly believed it was a vow they could keep. In the distance thunder rumbled, sounding like Fate's laughter as dark clouds moved to steal the moonlight from the sky.

Chapter One

"I have a tidbit of gossip guaranteed to curl your hair," Janice Kirkwood exclaimed as she sank down opposite Belinda Connor in the diner booth at the Great Day Diner.

Belinda grinned at her best friend. "You're always promising gossip to curl my hair." She touched the heavy braid that fell forward over her shoulder. "So far you haven't had much luck."

"This will do it." Janice paused for dramatic effect. "I just heard Derek Walker is back in town."

Belinda felt the blood leave her face as myriad emotions flowed through her. Even the mention of his name caused her breath to catch in her chest, an ache to pierce through her heart.

She reached for her glass and took a sip of water, hoping she kept any emotion from her expression. "That's interesting, but you didn't curl my hair."

"Interesting?" Janice frowned. "I expected to get a little more of a rise out of you. I mean, you and Derek did have a thing between you for a while."

"You dated him, too," Belinda reminded her friend.

Janice waved her hand dismissively. "That was ae-ons ago, when we were nothing but mere kids. We all know those puppy love romances don't count."

"Yeah, well my little romance with Derek didn't count, either. It was just a summer thing," Belinda replied, irritated by the edge of bitterness in her tone. "Besides, it's all ancient history now."

"Three years isn't such ancient history," Janice protested. She eyed Belinda with speculation. "I heard he's worth a small fortune, that since he left here he's done some investing or something and made oodles of money."

"Good for him," Belinda replied, grateful when the waitress appeared at their table to take their lunch orders.

"Now, tell me you're going to help me with the decorations for the Harvest Moon Dance," Janice said when the waitress had departed.

"Oh, I don't know. To tell you the truth, I hadn't planned to come to the dance."

Janice's brown eyes snapped in protest. "You have to come. In fact, I was counting on you helping me at the refreshment table, like you did last year."

Belinda frowned thoughtfully. The Harvest Moon Dance was a high point on the annual Cheyenne so-cial calendar. Held in a local community center, the event brought together neighbors from the ranches on the outskirts of town for an evening of merriment be-fore the harsh Wyoming winter set in.

"Come on, you know we always have fun," Janice encouraged. "Besides, you spend far too much time cooped up at the ranch."

Belinda laughed. "It's called work, Janice. You should try it sometime."

"I work," Janice protested.

"Being in charge of decorations for the Harvest Moon Dance and on the refreshment committee of the Womens' Club aren't exactly real jobs," Belinda chided.

Janice shrugged. "It's as real as I want to get. You know my dream is to marry a wealthy rancher and spend the rest of my life satisfying his every sexual whim." She laughed as a blush reddened Belinda's cheeks.

As the two friends ate their lunch, Belinda found herself thinking about what Janice had said. Once Belinda'd had dreams. Dreams of love, of marrying a rancher and filling a house with children, dreams she'd shared with Derek. But those dreams had gone up in flames, charred within the harsh clutch of lonely despair, leaving nothing but ashes and the bitter remnants of what might have been behind.

And now he was back.

She didn't want to see him, and yet knew the odds were good that eventually they'd run into each other. After all, the Walker place bordered the Connor ranch. However the Walker place was in ruins. The house had burned three years ago and now weeds choked the area that had once been neatly tended lawn.

"You sure got quiet," Janice said, breaking into Belinda's thoughts.

"Just thinking," Belinda replied, picking listlessly at the salad in front of her.

"About Derek?" Janice eyed her slyly.

"Of course not," Belinda lied. "I told you, that's long over. Ancient history. I have absolutely no feelings for him whatsoever."

Janice speared a French fry, then looked at Belinda again. "Then you wouldn't mind if I tried to renew an old high school romance with him?"

A pang shot through Belinda's heart at Janice's question. She ignored it and forced a smile. "You certainly don't need my permission. Derek doesn't belong to me. He never did." The pang deepened.

Thank goodness nobody knew just how serious Belinda and Derek's summer romance had been three years ago. Although everyone had known they were dating, nobody had known the depth of their passion, the utter abandonment she'd known in his arms. Thank goodness nobody had known, leaving Belinda a modicum of dignity now.

"We'll see," Janice continued. "I mean, I haven't even seen him yet. He might be married…or fat…or bald." She sighed. "So, are you going to help me with the refreshments and the decorations for the dance or not?" she asked with the lightning-quick change of topic that made conversation with her never boring.

"Yes, I'll help you," Belinda relented. She knew Janice had the tenacity of a pit bull and would hound her until she gave in. Might as well save both of them the energy by agreeing now.

"Great. Come to the community center next Saturday morning at ten to decorate. I figure it will take us about four to six hours, but we'll be out of there in plenty of time to make ourselves gorgeous for the dance that night."

Within minutes the two had finished lunch. "I've got to get home. I promised Abby I'd baby-sit Cody this afternoon." She smiled at thoughts of her six-year-old nephew.

"I thought Maria usually baby-sat Cody when Abby needed a sitter," Janice said, referring to the Connor cook and housekeeper.

"She quit last week. Her sister has been ill for quite a while and she decided to stop working and nurse her sister full-time. Anyway, Abby and Luke have an appointment to talk to our banker and I promised to look after Cody."

Janice frowned sympathetically. "Things still rough financially?"

Belinda nodded. "Abby and Colette are talking about taking a trip to California in the next couple of weeks. Seems there're several businessmen out there looking to make some investments. We're hoping to get them to invest in our place."

"Whatever happened to the dude ranch idea? I thought you were taking guests at the ranch to try to make extra money."

Belinda frowned, remembering the months of work and the renovations undertaken in an effort to turn the ranch into a successful vacation spot. "We realized we were spending more than we were making on the venture." She sighed. "Our best hope right now is those investors."

"What will you all do if they decide not to invest?"

Belinda's heart grew heavy at Janice's question. "Sell out. Start someplace new. I don't really know. We haven't talked much about what we'll do if we have to sell. I gotta go. Call me.''

As Belinda drove home she thought of her friendship with Janice. They had gone through high school together as nodding acquaintances, then Belinda had left Cheyenne, going to Kansas City to escape memories of Derek.

She'd come home five months ago and one afternoon she and Janice had found themselves sharing space in a dentist's office waiting room.

While they'd waited for their appointments a friendship had blossomed that had only deepened with each day that had since passed. Belinda's sisters referred to the two as Mutt and Jeff. Not only were Belinda and Janice unlike physically, their entire backgrounds and life-styles were totally diverse, as well.

She clenched her fingers on the steering wheel. Derek was back. Derek, with his laughing brown eyes and hair the color of wheat. Derek, with his lips of fire and caresses that had been her introduction to passion.

Despite their close proximity in growing up on neighboring ranches, Derek had never looked twice at her until he'd returned home for the summer after his junior year at college. That summer, a spark had ignited between them, a spark that quickly grew into an intense flame.

And now he was back. Derek, with his laughing eyes and golden hair. Derek, with his lying heart and false promises.

Belinda shook her head, as if to dislodge thoughts of him. She didn't want to think about him or the love she'd once felt for him. She certainly didn't want to see him ever again.

As the ranch came into view, her heart constricted with new worry. She and her sisters were about to lose the ranch. Unless something drastic happened, they figured they had less than six months of hanging on before having to sell out.

Belinda parked in front of the long ranch house and bounded out of the car. She wasn't sure exactly what time Abby and Luke's appointment at the bank was and hoped they weren't waiting for her.

She found both her older sister, Abby, and her younger sister, Colette, in the kitchen with their husbands, finishing up lunch. Abby's six-year-old son Cody was feeding Colette's five-month-old daughter, Brook. A mixture of pureed plums and rice cereal decorated the little girl's face.

The warmth of the domestic scene caused a renewed burst of loneliness, of isolation, to shoot through Belinda. She shrugged it off and joined her family at the table.

"Where did you take off to?" Colette asked. "You missed most of lunch."

"I met Janice for lunch at the diner," Belinda replied. "She talked me into helping with the decorations for the Harvest Moon Dance."

Abby smiled. "That woman needs a real job."

"That's exactly what I told her," Belinda said with a laugh. "But you know Janice, the last thing she wants to do is any real work."

"Hmm, too bad her parents don't want to invest in our ranch. It would be a lot cheaper than paying their daughter's keep," Abby observed.

"Somehow I can't imagine Janice Kirkwood mucking out stables," Abby's husband Luke said, making them all laugh at the ridiculous image his words conjured.

"What time is your appointment at the bank?" Belinda asked.

"We got canceled," Luke said. "We're rescheduled for tomorrow."

"So you don't need me to baby-sit Cody?"

"I don't need no baby-sitter. I'm not a baby," Cody exclaimed.

"No. It looks like you've got a free afternoon," Abby replied.

Belinda stood. "Then I think I'll take a little walk, try to exercise off some of my lunch." She waved a quick goodbye, then escaped out the back door.

Spring and summer had brought love to Colette and Abby, and their newlywed status still shone on their faces. While Belinda was thrilled that her sisters had found love, their happiness sharpened Belinda's feeling of aloneness. And now autumn was in the air, but Belinda knew the change of season would bring no life changes for her.

She buttoned her cardigan against the chill in the air and breathed deeply of the sharp, sweet scents of home. Late-blooming flowers scented the air and combined with the fragrance of soil and sun.

Relative silence filled the air. No workers bustled about, mending fences or herding horses and cattle. Because of financial constraints, the Connors were down to a skeleton crew; five hired men doing the work of dozens.

Roger Eaton, one of the few workers who'd remained at the ranch since spring, waved to her as he exited the barn. She waved back and continued walking toward the large tree that stood on a small rise in the distance.

The dragon tree. It blazed in glorious autumn colors, the fall foliage shaped like a mythical fire-breathing dragon. She always felt safe beneath the shade of the dragon tree. The large oak, scarred by a long-ago lightning strike, battered by winter winds and outlasting summer droughts, had endured unbowed for as long as Belinda could remember.

Beneath this tree the three sisters had mourned the deaths of their parents, and beneath its loving branches both of her sisters had exchanged their wedding vows.

She'd always associated her family with the tree. Survivors in a land that could sometimes be harsh. But surviving was becoming more difficult.

She frowned, deciding she was too restless to sit. Instead she walked away from the tree, in the direction of the old Walker place.

Derek was back. The words reverberated in her head, creating a wistful ache and a burning resentment that went right to her soul. Why was he back? What possible reason did he have for returning after three long years away?

The house where he once had lived with his parents was gone, only the stone chimney stood like a lone sentinel to guard the ashes of ruin and the concrete foundation that remained.

Weeds grew waist-high, mingling with wildflowers that dotted the landscape with fragrant beauty. A grove of trees to the left of where the house once stood beckoned to Belinda, but she ignored the lure of bittersweet memories.

She sank down onto the concrete foundation. It had been there, on a starlit night amid the sweet-smelling grass beneath the trees that she and Derek had first made love. There that she had pledged her love to him and promised him forever. He'd promised the same. Lies. All lies.

"Hello, Belinda."

She jumped with a gasp as a tall figure stepped out of the shadows of the trees. "Derek!" Shock rippled through her. She wasn't ready for this, wasn't prepared to see him again, and yet her eyes drank in his presence as he stepped into the sunshine.

He's changed, she thought. Although, the changes weren't dramatic, nothing she could specifically put her finger on. His hair was still colored with the kiss of the sun and his features were still the same clean-cut, well-defined ones that had made him a heartthrob in high school. Golden Boy. That's what all the girls had called him behind his back. He'd been a star athlete, liked by his male friends, lusted after by the females at school.

But his eyes were different now. Darker. Lacking the warmth and humor they had once retained.

As he advanced toward her, she noticed he had a slight limp, although the limp did nothing to dispel his utter masculinity.

His chambray shirt hugged the width of his shoulders and his jeans rode low on slender hips. He looked much the same as he had the last time she'd seen him. Except for the hardness in his gaze.

"I—I heard you were back in town." She finally found her voice.

"And so I am."

"Going to be here long?" she asked.

He kicked at a charred piece of wood. "I'm re-building the house. I plan to make my home here."

His words once again sent shock riveting through her. Even though Janice had told her he was back in town, she'd never anticipated that he intended to stay, to make a permanent home here.

"So, how have you been, Belinda?" He stepped closer to her, bringing with him an evocative scent of musky cologne and maleness.

What do you care? You promised to love me forever, then disappeared out of my life without a backward glance. She swallowed against the old resentment and flashed him a bright smile. "Good. Great, actually."

His gaze remained on her, dark and probing. "I heard your sisters got married."

She nodded. What she wanted to do was run away, distance herself from him and all the memories that suffused her. But she refused to show him how his presence affected her, that she bore any scars at all from their brief and passionate affair.

"What about you? Any marriage plans in your near future?"

She forced a laugh. "Heavens, no. I'm having too much fun to tie myself down to anyone right now." She didn't tell him there were no marriage plans in her distant future, either. She wouldn't trust in love again. Never again. Not ever.

What she'd shared with Derek had been so intense, and had resulted in a loss too enormous. A loss she'd suffered alone. Not even her sisters had known the enormous penalty she'd paid for loving Derek.

"You look good, Belinda. Just as I remembered

you.'' He took a step closer to her and she backed away, afraid he might touch her, afraid he'd manage to somehow pierce through the veil of anger and resentment that protected her heart.

She wrapped her arms around herself. "I heard you've been quite successful since leaving here."

He eased himself down onto the foundation where she had been sitting when he'd first appeared. "Yes, I've managed to amass what some would refer to as a small fortune. It seems I have what appears to be a remarkable aptitude for playing the stock market. I started with some of the money Mom and Dad got from the insurance settlement on the fire here. Before long my investments doubled, then tripled." He shrugged. "I got lucky."

"You could choose to live anywhere. Why come back here?"

He looked up at her, his eyes shining with a fierce determination, a whisper of dangerous anger that nearly stole her breath away. "There are two reasons why I've come back here, Belinda. Three years ago somebody set fire to my house. It was a deliberate act and it destroyed my home, my parents' lives and my life. I'm here to find out who did it and why."

Belinda gasped. "I never knew the fire was deliberately set. Are you sure it wasn't just an accident?"

He hesitated a moment, a pulse throbbing at his temple. "I can't be sure until I check the records, but it's something I have to follow up on."

"How are you going to find out who might have done it after all this time?" Belinda asked.

Some of the anger in his gaze dissipated. "I don't know."

"Sounds like a fool's errand to me. It's been three years. You can't know for sure somebody really did it on purpose. Besides, why on earth would somebody do such a thing?"

"That's what I'm here to find out."

"You should just forget about it, get on with your life. It's best just to forget the past and move on." She averted her gaze from his, sounding stronger than she felt.

"Is that what you've done?" he asked softly.

For a moment his question hung in the air, filling her heart with powerful emotions and the heartache of years gone by.

She met his gaze once again, this time raising her chin with a touch of bravado. "That's definitely what I've done."

He stood and took a step toward her. Once again his familiar scent wrapped around her, reminding her of good times...and that horrible time that followed. "That's too bad," he said softly. "You haven't asked me what the second thing is that I came back for."

"And what is that?"

He stared at her for another long moment before answering. "You."

Chapter Two

"Me?" She stared at him in shocked surprise. "It appears you've come back on two fool's errands," she said coldly.

He eyed her speculatively. "I understand you and your sisters are about to lose your ranch, that you're interested in acquiring some investors. You need money and I need a temporary wife."

"What are you talking about? Why do you need a temporary wife?"

He leaned against a tree trunk and folded his arms across his chest. His eyes were dark, shuttered against any invasion. "You remember my older brother, Mike?" She nodded and he continued. "Two months ago he and his wife were killed in a car accident. I've petitioned the courts for custody of their two children, but it seems the judge is rather old-fashioned and thinks I should be married. I need a wife and you need money."

"That's crazy," Belinda exclaimed, her heart thudding a wild rhythm. "You can't buy me."

"I don't want to buy you. I just want to buy some of your time." Once again his eyes were cold and distant as he gazed at her. "Don't make the mistake of thinking this would be a marriage of passion or of love. Rather it would simply be a marriage of convenience. Once my adoption of the kids is finalized, you'd be free to go your own way."

"Why me? I'm sure there are dozens of women who would be thrilled to be married to you."

"Because I have something you need, and somebody else might expect some kind of emotional investment. This would be strictly a business merger, without our emotions involved."

"And in return?" Belinda couldn't believe how coldly he outlined his plans for a marriage.

"I'll invest whatever you think necessary to allow you to keep your ranch running."

"I still don't understand why me. There are women who'd marry you for cold, hard cash and sign an agreement to divorce you later."

"I'm aware of that," he said easily. "But I know you. I trust you. And I know you're an honorable woman and will abide by the terms." He held up a hand as she started to speak. "Think about it. You don't have to give me an answer right now. Just think about it. Belinda, we need each other."

"There's nothing to think about," she retorted. She'd needed him three years ago and he'd been nowhere to be found. He'd left Cheyenne and never looked back, leaving her to deal with the casualty of their summer affair and her love for him. "I've got to get back home." She turned to leave, but hesitated when he called after her.

"I won't give up easily."

She didn't answer, but continued on her way. Too

many emotions assaulted her, overloading her brain and making rational thought nearly impossible.

Memories of the past battled with realities of the present. Once upon a time she would have rejoiced at Derek's talk of marriage. But this was no fairy tale, and the love she'd once felt for Derek had transformed to a bitter anger.

Besides, he hadn't talked of love or passion. His offer was strictly based in a need for a wife, and a cold detachment had shone from his eyes.

She loved her sisters, loved the ranch. But there had to be another way to save it. A marriage of convenience to Derek was an absurd idea. No matter how desperate she was to help save the ranch, her heart could never countenance such a thing.

DEREK WATCHED HER walk away, the afternoon sunshine flirting with the golden braid that hung down her back. For three years her features had remained etched in his mind, taunting him with the memory of her wholesome beauty, reminding him of love found, then lost.

He wondered if she'd seen the lies in his eyes, recognized the subterfuge hidden there. He hadn't lied about one thing: what he'd offered her had nothing to do with love. He'd never risk his heart again. In the past three years he'd learned to believe in the power of money, and discount the longevity of love.

He turned at the sound of a pickup approaching, a smile curving his lips as he recognized the beat-up vehicle that pulled to a stop by the house foundation. The big, burly man who got out of the truck looked exactly like he had in high school and college. He and Derek had grown up together and had been best friends.

"Bear, you old coot. You haven't changed a bit since last time I saw you," Derek exclaimed as he clapped his friend on the back.

Teddy King, nicknamed Bear for his build, grinned at Derek. Although the two had talked often on the phone over the past three years, they hadn't seen each other since the night before the fire that destroyed Derek's home.

Bear wrapped him in a hug that nearly squeezed the breath from him. "God, Derek, I'm so damned glad to have you back in town. My men should be arriving soon, but I wanted a few minutes by myself with you before we start to work."

Bear owned a construction company and Derek had hired his old friend to rebuild the house. "It's good to be back," Derek said. Surveying the area that had once been his home, he leaned against a tree trunk. "You still think you can get the house up in a couple of weeks?"

"Weather permitting and as long as you're willing to pay for overtime, yes."

Derek nodded in satisfaction.

Bear put the tailgate of his truck down and motioned for Derek to join him. "So, how's it feel to be back?" he asked.

Derek sat next to Bear, flashing him a grin as the big man opened a cooler and withdrew two colas. "Thanks." He popped the top and took a deep swallow. "It feels good." He took another drink and for a moment silence grew between the two men. "I have nightmares about the fire." Derek broke the silence, remembering that night of hell when he'd awakened to find fire surrounding him. "I wake up drenched in sweat, fighting the fire in my dreams. I've been told the best way to exorcise monsters is to face them. So, here I am." But it hadn't been the memory of the fire that had brought him back. He frowned, realizing he was building a pyramid of lie upon lie.

"I just hope you get a chance to face the son-of-a-bitch that set the fire," Bear said.

"I plan to talk to Junior tomorrow, see if I can get all the old records from the initial investigation," Derek said, referring to the sheriff. "I talked to Belinda."

Bear raised his bushy eyebrows. "And?"

"And let's say she didn't exactly pounce on my offer." Derek had told Bear that he intended to propose to Belinda in an effort to gain custody of his niece and nephew. Until Derek sniffed around, discovered exactly what was going on, he didn't intend to tell anyone, even his best friend, what had really prompted him back here to Belinda.

"You didn't really expect her to fall to her knees in gratitude, did you?" Bear asked wryly. "You told me you wrote her a pretty cold kiss-off note after the fire."

Derek steeled himself against any remorse that might creep into his thoughts. "It was for the best. At the time I wasn't sure I was going to live, wasn't sure I wouldn't be a cripple the rest of my life. I'd rather have her hatred than her pity." For a moment his mind flashed with an image of he and Belinda making love, of her hands stroking him with loving caresses as she told him he was the most beautiful man she'd ever dreamed of knowing.

"Yeah, but if you need a wife, I'd think a woman who doesn't hate you would be a little better bet," Bear said.

"Her hatred of me is exactly what makes her perfect for what I want. I need a temporary wife, one who can pretend in public, but who has no desire to make the facade a reality. When you told me the Connors were having a tough time hanging on to their ranch, it presented the perfect opportunity for me to get what I want, and give Belinda what she needs."

Bear shook his head with a rueful smile. "I still think that fire melted some of your brain cells, but I'm not the one you have to convince. Belinda is."

Derek nodded. "I know." He turned at the sound of approaching trucks. As Bear's team of workers began to arrive, Derek clapped him on the back once again. "You do your job and build me a house in record time and leave Belinda to me."

Bear grinned. "Don't worry. I'm not about to interfere with your love life. You always did have all the luck with the ladies."

As Bear went to greet his men, Derek finished his cola and clenched his fist to crush the can. Yeah, he'd always had plenty of luck with the ladies, he thought bitterly. Unfortunately the flames that had destroyed his home so many years before had also obliterated his capacity to love...to be loved.

There were only two people on earth he cared about. His four-year-old nephew and five-year-old niece, who resided in a foster home awaiting Uncle

Derek to rescue them and bring them to his house to live with him.

He'd received the first anonymous note about Belinda on the same day he'd met with the judge presiding over the custody hearing. When the judge had asked him about his marital status, Derek had known the children's fate hinged on his reply. He'd told the judge he was to be married to Belinda within the month and would have a stable, two-parent environment for the kids. It had been a foolish thing to say, but now his fate was intricately bound to her with a web of lies.

He couldn't tell Belinda the other reason he was here, didn't want to needlessly frighten her. He didn't want to tell her that he thought her life was in danger and he had returned here to find out who might want her dead.

He pushed off of the tailgate, his mind racing with possibilities. He had no idea who to suspect, what the motive might be. He only knew that for some reason the potential killer wanted him back here, wanted him to play a role in whatever deadly game was about to unfold. He intended to marry Belinda, keep her safe until he found out what the hell was going on. Marriage would give him a reason to be close to her every minute of every day. He had to convince her to marry him…her very life might depend on it.

BELINDA SAT in her car, reluctant to enter the community center where merriment spilled out the door with each person that went in. The rest of her family had left earlier to come to the Harvest Moon Dance, but Belinda had decided to drive herself. She wanted to be able to leave whenever she was ready without pulling her family away from the festivities.

She didn't do well at social gatherings. Abby and Colette both possessed a confident charm that made it easy for them to revel in crowds, but Belinda found that crowd-pleasing charm didn't come naturally to her.

There was another reason she was reluctant to join the fun. She knew Derek would be inside. It seemed he'd shadowed her all week long. Every time she turned around, she saw him in the distance, watching her like a hawk eyeing prey.

Still, it was ridiculous to sit in her car any longer. Janice would probably already be frantic, wondering where she was, and in their short friendship Belinda had learned that Janice's temper was an awesome thing to behold.

She got out of her car and walked toward the rear of the building, vowing to try to enjoy the evening no matter what. Drawing a deep breath, she stepped inside. Sights, smells and sounds immediately overwhelmed her. She and Janice and a handful of other people had worked all afternoon to transform the large sterile room into a fall festival. Bales of hay provided sitting niches. Plump pumpkins and colorful Indian corn complimented the scenery.

The scents of apple cider, homemade breads and cakes added to the people smells of perfume and fresh-scrubbed skin.

The noise level was tolerable...barely. A group of teenage boys who thought themselves country-western musicians had been hired to play for the night and they warmed up on the stage, producing a variety of guitar squeals and drumrolls.

Janice stood behind the refreshment table. Spying Belinda, she motioned her over with a wave of her hand. "Thank goodness you're here. I thought maybe you'd chickened out on me," she exclaimed as Belinda joined her. "Wow, you look terrific. Is that new?"

Belinda nodded and smoothed the skirt of the cinnamon-colored dress. "I couldn't resist it."

"How do you like mine?" Janice twirled to display the electric blue outfit she wore.

"It looks great, but you might want to watch bending over," Belinda observed, noting the plunging neckline that barely contained her friend's attributes.

Janice laughed. "You know what they say, in order to sell them you've got to display them."

"Any more of a display and you'll be arrested for indecent exposure," Belinda replied.

Janice laughed again. "Come on, help me cut up this pumpkin bread and put it on a platter."

Belinda worked efficiently, cutting up first the loaf of pumpkin bread, then doing the same with a loaf of banana bread. As she worked, she felt her skin prickle in sudden awareness, as if a lightning bolt was about to strike nearby.

She looked up and her gaze met Derek's. He leaned against the wall near the front door, arms folded across his broad chest. Although Bear stood next to him, chatting and grinning at each group of people that came in the door, Derek seemed to pay his friend no notice. His sole concentration appeared to be on Belinda.

For a long moment his gaze captured hers, his eyes holding hers prisoner. She felt as if she'd fallen into their dark depths, where memories of passion resided, memories of summer nights and heated caresses, of whispered promises and sighs of pleasure.

"You cut that any thinner, we might as well serve air."

Janice's voice snapped Belinda's attention from Derek to her task at hand. She realized she'd been cutting the bread into pieces too small to serve. "Sorry," she mumbled, and refocused her concentration on what she was doing.

Still her skin prickled and she knew Derek watched her, but she didn't dare look in his direction. She didn't want to encourage any interaction between them whatsoever.

"Well, he hasn't gotten fat," Janice said. Belinda knew immediately who she was talking about.

"I know, I spoke to him a couple of days ago." Belinda looked at her friend. "He had some crazy idea about the two of us marrying."

"What?" Janice's eyes widened. She pulled Belinda away from the table, back into a corner. "Tell all."

Belinda frowned, regretting what had blurted out of her without volition. "It was just some crazy idea he had. Seems he needs a temporary wife to get custody of his niece and nephew."

"Are you going to do it?"

"Of course not," Belinda scoffed. "I told you last week, my relationship with Derek is the past."

"Obviously he doesn't feel the same way," Janice observed. She looked across the room and Belinda knew she eyed Derek, but Belinda didn't follow her gaze.

"Come on, let's get back to the table. I see people drifting over for apple cider."

For the next hour or so Belinda was grateful that the room was warm and people thirsty. At least while she served refreshments she found it easier to keep thoughts of Derek at bay.

The band began playing and the floor filled up with twirling couples. The music stirred rhythm in everyone. Even Belinda found her foot tapping to the lively beat. She smiled as she spied Cody dancing with Abby, his features in painful concentration as he maneuvered his mother around the floor.

Roger Eaton had his hands full trying to keep up with Janice who resembled an electric blue flame as she gyrated to the music. Belinda smiled to herself, watching the ranch hand ogle Janice. Poor Roger, Janice would eat him alive.

"Hi, Belinda."

Belinda smiled at the solidly built cowboy in front of her. "Hey, Bulldog, you having a good time?"

He nodded, his moon face beaming with a smile. "I gotta new shirt to wear." He smoothed his big hands down the front of the checkered shirt.

"It's very nice," Belinda replied. "You look real handsome."

He blushed, the tips of his ears shining bright red. Affectionate warmth spread through Belinda for Bulldog. With his Herculean build and mind of a child, he had enough heart to more than compensate for any lack of learning ability.

"I was thinking of asking Rhonda Grover to dance,

but I'm kinda scared. I never danced with a woman before.''

Belinda looked over to where Rhonda sat alone on a bale of hay. The young woman, though painfully shy, was known for having a sweet nature. ''Why don't you have a little practice dance with me, then maybe you wouldn't be so afraid of asking Rhonda,'' Belinda suggested.

Bulldog smiled again. ''That's a good idea. I always need to practice stuff.''

Belinda showed Bulldog where to put his hands and they swayed to the music. Although the beat was fast, their feet barely moved. Initial tenseness knotted his body, but after a few moments he began to relax.

''You're doing very well,'' Belinda said.

''This ain't so hard.'' He frowned. ''You think Rhonda will notice…you know, my face?''

Belinda eyed the big cowboy who had become as much a part of her family as her sisters' husbands. Although the fire at their ranch had been more than two months ago, Bulldog's singed eyebrows had just started to grow back. That, combined with a residual redness, gave his face a rather startling appearance.

''I'm sure Rhonda has heard about the fire and what you did. She'll just think you have a hero's face.''

A beatific smile once again lit his features. ''A hero's face. That's nice.''

''Can I cut in?'' Derek's voice interrupted Bulldog's rhythm and he stumbled and stepped squarely on Belinda's foot.

''It's all right,'' Belinda assured Bulldog as he

gazed at her in horror. "Stepping on toes often happens in dancing." She studiously ignored Derek.

"I'd like a turn at stepping on her toes," Derek said to the big man.

Belinda wanted to protest, to tell Bulldog she didn't want to dance with Derek. She didn't want to feel his arms around her, but she also didn't want to make a scene. "It's okay, Bulldog," she finally said reluctantly. "Why don't you go on over and ask Rhonda to dance? You'll be fine."

Bulldog looked from Derek to Belinda, as if assuring himself that everything was all right. "Don't you step on her feet too hard now," he said to Derek, then turned and walked off in the direction of Rhonda.

As Derek took her in his arms, the fast-beat music segued to a slower popular tune. Belinda held herself stiff, unyielding against his achingly familiar embrace.

His flannel shirt was soft beneath her fingertips, but the muscles beneath were firm, evoking memories of how that sun-bronzed flesh had felt naked beneath her caresses.

"You look lovely tonight," he said.

She tilted her head back to look at his face. "If you think flattery will make me agree to your crazy scheme, you're sadly mistaken."

He smiled, although again she noticed no humor touched the darkness of his eyes. "I don't use flattery to manipulate. It was a simple statement, intended at face value. You do look lovely."

"Thank you," she answered stiffly, hating herself for being unable to control the blush that heated her cheeks.

"What happened to Bulldog's face? Looks like he got a bad burn."

"He did. You remember Rusty, our foreman?" He nodded and she continued. "A couple of months ago Rusty tried to burn down our house with Luke and Abby inside. Bulldog helped them get out and in the process suffered some burns."

She immediately felt Derek's body tense and guessed what he was thinking about. "I'm pretty sure Rusty would have had no reason to start the fire that burned your family out."

"Yeah, you're probably right. Still, think I'll mention the possibility when I talk to Junior. I've been so busy with the rebuilding of the house this past week I haven't had a chance to get into the investigation of the fire."

As the music stopped she tried to move away from his embrace, but he held her tight. "I heard through the grapevine that the bank denied Abby's request for extended credit."

Belinda sighed. "Sometimes I think the only thing that works well around here is the damned grapevine."

Derek laughed, the deep sound wrapping around her with a renewed burst of memories. "You should know by now the grapevine is one of the hazards of small community living."

"Well I certainly don't want to give them anything else to talk about, so if you'll excuse me." She managed to extricate herself from his hold and step away.

"Belinda, my offer still stands. I could make things easier on you and your sisters if you'd agree to my terms."

"My price for selling my soul is much higher than the worth of our ranch," she retorted, then whirled around and stomped off the dance floor.

DEREK WATCHED her as she made her way through the crowd back to the refreshment table. Her perfume lingered after her, eddying in his head with dizzying familiarity.

He'd forgotten the scent of her, the sweet smell of honeysuckle that had always been her trademark. He hadn't lied, she looked beautiful. The rust-colored dress brought out the blue of her eyes and emphasized her fading summer tan.

He couldn't lie to himself, part of his reason for coming back here had been his haunting memories of Belinda. He'd loved her once. Desperately. With all the emotion a twenty-two-year-old could maintain. But that had been when he'd been capable of love.

Besides, at almost twenty years old, Belinda had professed her love for him, had promised to love him forever, but she certainly hadn't fought very hard to keep their love intact. She'd allowed him to walk out of her life without a whimper.

As he walked back to where Bear leaned against the wall, Derek saw Henry Carsworth approaching him. He stifled a groan.

Derek had first met the short, squat man when he'd shown up at Derek's mother's and father's home not long after the fire had destroyed their ranch. He'd indicated an interest in buying the property. At that time Derek's father had hoped to rebuild and turned Carsworth's offer down. Throughout the past three years Carsworth had been as tenacious as a tick, writing or showing up from time to time with a new offer to buy.

"Walker." Henry greeted Derek with a friendly nod. "Heard you were back in town."

"You heard right." Derek eyed the pseudo cowboy with a touch of amusement. When Derek had first met him, he'd been in a three-piece suit and looked every inch the successful California businessman. Obviously at some point in the passing years Henry Carsworth had gone Western.

His expensive jeans were held around his bulk by a leather belt with a buckle as big as a dinner plate. Custom-made cowboy boots added several inches to his minimal height and a sprout of dark hair decorated the space between his nose and upper lip.

"I guess you finally got your wish and bought a place out here," Derek said.

"Actually, I'm living at the Manor Boarding House right now, although I'm hopeful I'll be settling into my own place before winter sets in." Carsworth grinned, the bloodless smile of a businessman first, an affable cowboy second. "'Course if you weren't so damned stubborn, I'd already be settled in here."

Derek smiled thinly. "Our property has been in our family for several generations. Even if I hadn't decided to rebuild, I'd have never sold."

"Your place and the Connors' ranch have the best grazing land around here. Yours might not be on the market, but I don't think the Connors are going to be able to hang on much longer." He withdrew a fat cigar from his breast pocket.

"I wouldn't count the Connors down and out yet," Derek replied.

Henry nodded. "Those Connor women are tough broads, but they can't fight reality. They got the best grazing land, and not enough cattle to make it pay. Financially, they're a mess." He paused long enough to light the cigar. He drew deeply on it, then released a smoke ring. He watched for a moment as the ring climbed in the air, then turned back to Derek and grinned. "I can be a patient man. I don't like it, but I can be patient. And I have a feeling if I just wait a while, the Connor ranch will be mine." He clapped Derek on the back. "See you around, neighbor," he said, then walked toward the refreshment table.

Tough broads. Derek looked over to where Belinda was now dancing with Sheriff Junior Blanchard. Of the three sisters, Belinda had always struck Derek as the least tough. When in the company of her sisters, she seemed to disappear, unwilling to compete with Abby's confidence and Colette's vivaciousness.

"Still waters," his mother had said about Belinda.

At the time Derek had smiled, believing he knew Belinda's heart, her soul, like no other man ever would. But that was a long time ago.

He no longer knew what was in her heart, in her soul, except that she'd retained a bitter resentment toward him. *That's what you wanted,* a small voice whispered inside him.

It was a curious paradox. He wanted to marry her, to protect her from harm, but he had to maintain the resentment that would forever keep her heart from his, the resentment that would make it easy to walk away from each other when the need for the marriage passed.

His gaze shifted from Belinda back to Henry Carsworth. Somehow he wasn't surprised Henry was here. When Derek had met him in California, the little man had displayed an absolute obsession to live in or around the Cheyenne area.

Would Carsworth's desire to live on a ranch in Wyoming extend to murder to gain what he wanted? Was it possible Carsworth intended to kill Belinda in some twisted scheme to get the Connor ranch?

He looked back at Belinda, who was once again dancing with Bulldog. He knew his idea for a marriage of convenience was crazy, but he didn't know what else to do. Somebody wanted him to know she was in danger. Somebody expected him to come running back to protect her. He could never allow himself to love her again, but he couldn't stand by and do nothing while somebody tried to harm her.

Somebody had threatened to kill her, and Derek wanted to make sure whoever it was had to come through him first.

Chapter Three

Belinda breathed a sigh of relief as she finished washing the large punch bowl and placed it on the shelf in the kitchen of the community building. Although the band had agreed to play for another hour, the refreshment committee had decided to stop serving and contend with the cleanup.

"Whew, that's it," Janice said as she entered the compact kitchen area. "I think I'm ready to call it a night."

"Me, too." Belinda pulled her car keys from her purse. "Is your car still in the shop? You need a ride home?"

"Yes, my car is still in the shop, but I talked Daddy into letting me take one off the lot, so I've got my own wheels for the night." She flashed a quick smile. "There are definite benefits to having a father who owns a used car lot."

Belinda returned the smile. "I'm out of here. Call me sometime this week. We'll have lunch."

Waving goodbye to her friend, Belinda slipped out the back door and walked around the building to her car. Grateful to be out of the noise, away from the crowd, she drew in a deep breath of the chill autumn night air.

More than anything, she was grateful to be away from Derek's dark and steady gaze. His gaze had followed her throughout the evening, probing... haunting...demanding her attention.

Damn him for coming back here and disrupting her life with his very presence. Damn him for even mentioning his crazy marriage scheme, a scheme that refused to vacate her mind no matter how she tried to forget it.

She sighed tiredly as she turned off onto the rural road that would take her home. She hit her high beams to illuminate the narrow, tree-lined road, still struggling against thoughts of Derek.

In that brief moment when they'd danced together, she'd realized a sudden truth. As she'd felt his heartbeat against her own, as his scent had surrounded her with evocative familiarity, she'd realized it was possible to hate and desire at the same time.

She'd always believed that passion—desire—grew from love, but in that moment of being held by Derek, she'd realized it was possible for one to have little to do with the other.

Looking in her rearview mirror, she saw the headlights of another car approaching fast behind her. Too fast. Within moments the car's high beams glared in her mirror and nearly blinded her. "Jerk," she muttered, and flipped up her mirror to diffuse the glare.

She frowned as the car rode up behind her, so close the headlights disappeared altogether and she felt a thud of bumper meeting bumper.

"Hey," she yelled, and pressed the gas pedal in an

attempt to gain some distance. But the car behind her accelerated, as well, once again striking her bumper with enough force to snap her head back painfully against her seat.

She tightened her grip on the steering wheel, swerving back and forth on the narrow road in an effort to evade whoever was behind her. But her pursuer remained with her.

The darkness of the night hid the car in anonymity. With no streetlights around and the moon shrouded by clouds, Belinda couldn't tell the make, model or color of the vehicle. However, it quickly became clear that the intention was to force her off the road, cause her to land in the ditch or perhaps hit one of the thick trees that lined the narrow road.

Her car was struck again, this time with enough force to send her into a near spin. She whirled the steering wheel in an effort to right the car and, over-compensating, felt her tires leave the road.

She screamed. Dark silhouettes of trees flashed in front of her. Branches slapped at the car. Brush screeched against the undercarriage as she fought to maintain control. The car smacked into a tree and Belinda snapped forward then backward, saved only by her seat belt from careering through the wind-shield.

Adrenaline pumped inside her as ragged breaths escaped through her lips. The engine died on impact and the sudden silence seemed to amplify her gasps for breath. Belinda unfastened the seat belt and whirled around to look at the road behind her.

Her attacker was still there…sitting on the road like a menacing shadow. Who was it? Why was this happening? Questions swirled in her mind as she stared at her pursuer. Unsure what might happen next, she eased down her window and kept her gaze focused on the car. She could hear the motor, a slight miss in the rhythm.

She narrowed her gaze, trying desperately to catch a glimpse of something—anything—that would identify the car or driver. Without warning, the engine revved, backfired, and the car shot off.

It wasn't until Belinda saw a pickup pull up and a man jump out that she realized that's what had caused the car to leave. And it wasn't until she heard Derek's voice that she realized the pickup was his. "Everyone all right in there?" he yelled.

He raced toward her, his tall figure visible in the glow from the moon. She started to get out of the car, but realized she couldn't. The adrenaline that had surged through her moments before was gone, leaving her shaken and weak.

Derek wrenched the car door open. "My God...Belinda. Are you all right?" His voice held a frantic tone that instantly caused tears to spring to her eyes.

"I'm okay..." A sob welled up inside, pressing thickly into her throat.

Derek helped her out and immediately pulled her into his arms. "Are you sure you're all right?"

She nodded, unable to speak as the horror of the situation swept through her. Tears came faster, blurring her vision. For a long moment Derek said nothing. He held her tight against his chest, his hands moving up and down her back as if to assure himself she was all there.

All feelings of past animosity fell aside as Belinda burrowed closer against him, needing his warmth, the security of his embrace to chase away the chills that still shivered through her.

She pulled away from him only when she realized how desperately she wanted to remain cradled in his arms. She walked around to the front of her car, staring in dismay at the damage. Steam hissed into the air from the busted radiator and the front end of the car had crumpled into itself beneath the force of the collision. There was no way she'd be able to drive it home.

"Want to tell me what happened?" Derek asked. "I came over the rise and saw headlights off the road and another car tearing away."

"I—I'm not sure what happened. All I know is some crazy nut decided to play bumper cars with me."

"Surely it was just an accident. Probably whoever was driving that car had too much to drink." An edge in his voice intensified his comment.

Belinda shivered and wrapped her arms around herself. "I—I don't know. Maybe," she replied, although her heart knew different. There was no way this was an accident. Perhaps the driver had been drunk, but there was no way to mistake what had happened. She'd been intentionally forced off the road.

Derek touched her arm. "It will take a tow truck to get your car out of here. Come on, let me take you home."

His fingers were warm...too warm on her bare skin. She jerked away from his touch. "No. If you'll just call Jake's Garage, I'll wait here for a tow truck." There was no way she wanted to get into the close confines of his pickup with him.

Despite the circumstances, in spite of the terror that still swirled inside her, she was far too conscious of the comfort she'd found in his arms, far too vulnerable to the desire she felt for him...a desire that refused to be quenched even beneath the weight of her bitterness.

"Don't be ridiculous," Derek replied. "There's no way I'm going to drive away and leave you here in the middle of nowhere to wait for Jake Watkins to tear himself away from the television to get out here." He paused and she saw a wry smile curve his lips. "What's the matter, Belinda? Afraid to be alone with me?"

"Don't be ridiculous," she snapped. She reached into her car and pulled the keys from the ignition, then placed them beneath the floor mat. "Okay. Let's go."

"When you get home you'd better call Sheriff Blanchard and make a report," Derek said as he started his pickup and headed toward the Connor ranch.

"I'm not sure there's any point. I don't suppose you got a good look at the car that hit mine?"

He shook his head. "Afraid not. All I saw were the taillights as it took off. You still should file a report. If nothing else, for insurance purposes."

"I suppose you're right." She cracked her window a couple of inches, hoping the chill night air would dispel the pleasant scent of him that filled the interior of the cab.

How was it possible to hate a man and yet feel so alive in his presence? she wondered. All her senses seemed heightened. The night appeared darker, the stars brighter, senses sharper. It had always been that way, and it irritated her that despite her heartache, the magic she'd always felt when he was around still remained.

Black magic, she scoffed inwardly. She'd always heard that a woman retained a special place in her heart for the man who was her first lover. But Belinda refused to entertain the idea that Derek held any part of her heart despite the fact that he'd been her first...and only lover.

"How's the house coming?" she asked to break the uncomfortable silence between them.

"Good. The frame is up and if the weather holds we should be able to finish up the outside work by the first of next week." His voice still held a taut edge that made her eye him curiously.

The illumination from the dashboard painted his face in a pale, amber light, emphasizing the strong lines and planes of his features. A knot pulsed at his jawline and she remembered that the one time she'd seen him angry, that throbbing knot had been the telltale signal of ire.

As if he felt her questioning gaze on him, he turned and smiled at her. "Since we have this time alone, I think we should talk about what's really important. Chocolate or vanilla?"

She stared at him blankly. "Chocolate or vanilla what?"

"Which do you prefer for our wedding cake?"

"There's not going to be a wedding cake," she returned, disturbed by the unevenness of her voice.

"Okay, we don't have to serve cake. But I really think we should have those different colored mints. People always like those mints."

"If I didn't know you better, I'd swear you manipulated that car to force me off the road just so you could trap me in this pickup and talk nonsense."

"It isn't nonsense," he countered. "It's the only thing that makes sense." He pulled up in front of the Connor ranch house, then turned to face her. "It's a way we can both get what we want."

"Derek, people don't marry for the kinds of reasons you're talking about. When I get married it will be for love, not for any other reason."

He laughed and shook his head. "Ah, Belinda, you're still waiting for some knight to ride up on a white steed and be your loving prince. Those are just fairy tales, Belinda. There are no princes, and love doesn't last."

It was difficult for Belinda to imagine this was the same man who'd once talked of stars and dreams. Again she was struck by how much he'd changed, that a core of hardness now resided in him that hadn't been there before.

Well, she had a core of hardness deep within her, too. But her stony heart was a direct result of his callousness and lies, of his false promises and betrayal. "All I really want, Derek, is for you to leave me alone. I don't want to be your temporary wife. I don't want to be anything to you."

She started out the passenger door. He grabbed her arm, stopping her escape. "Belinda, I need you to get the kids." His eyes bore into hers with an intensity that nearly stole her breath away.

She yanked out of his grip. "You don't understand, Derek. I don't care whether you need me or not."

He smiled. "Unless you want Henry Carsworth calling your place home, I'd say you need me every bit as much as I need you."

"The day I need you is the day Bulldog starts speaking French." She stepped down from the cab. "Go find somebody else to indulge you in this hare-brained scheme."

"Unfortunately, I told the judge your name. He's expecting you as my bride," he said. She stared at him in disbelief, appalled by his very nerve.

Again his eyes flared with an intense determination. "I can't tell you how important this is. I'm only asking for a couple of months of your time. Those kids need me, Belinda. And you're the only one that can help. I want to be a father."

She slammed the truck door and walked away, unable to speak as emotions raged inside her. She watched as his truck pulled away, the taillights disappearing into the darkness of the night.

Closing her eyes, she took a deep breath, trying to gain control of the turbulence within. She rarely consciously pulled up memories of those months alone in Kansas City, and she constantly fought intruding remembrances of being so alone, so afraid, as the pain of childbirth had racked her body.

Opening her eyes, she drew another breath, shoving away those painful memories that only created a renewed bitter taste in her mouth when she thought of Derek. She couldn't afford to dwell in past heart-

aches. She had something more urgent to consider…
Who had tried to run her off the road and why?

DEREK WENT A LITTLE WAY down the main road, then
turned off onto a narrow path that would take him by
the back of the Connor house. As he drove, he tightened his grip on the steering wheel, fighting an overwhelming sense of helplessness.

He'd shamelessly manipulated Belinda with his
talk of gaining custody of the children. But Belinda
had always had a soft spot in her heart for helpless
animals and little children, and he knew thoughts of
those children would prey on her mind and perhaps
catapult her into agreeing to a marriage.

He parked the truck in a grove of trees where he
had a perfect view of the back of the Connor house.
There was a single light on, shining out of the window he knew was Belinda's bedroom.

When the light went out, Derek's mind instantly
filled with a vision of Belinda in bed, her long hair
loose from its braided confines and flowing like honey
over the pillowcase.

He steeled himself against the evocative vision and
rubbed his thigh, the dull ache a constant reminder of
what would never be.

Part of what Belinda had loved about him years
before had been his physical appeal…a physical attractiveness now destroyed by ugly welts and scars.

The marriage scheme would provide him both the
opportunity to keep her safe until he found out who
intended to harm her and to get the kids he desperately wanted.

He'd spent the past week skulking around in the

shadows, trying to keep an eye on her. Marriage would make it easier.

The alternative was to tell somebody what he knew. Unfortunately he didn't know who to trust. Even her own family was suspect at the moment.

He cracked open the window, hoping the cool night air would help him stay awake to watch for any danger that might come in the darkness of night.

His heart thudded a dull rhythm of anxiety. He knew with dreadful certainty that Belinda's accident had been no accident. The game was in play and he had no clue who his opponents might be.

Chapter Four

For the first time in a long while, the entire Connor family sat at the kitchen table. Bedlam reigned as they passed pancakes and sausage links all around, everyone seeming to talk at once as they filled their plates.

It had been a week since the dance, a week of disappointments as they had exhausted all the avenues for a loan to keep the ranch going.

Tomorrow morning Belinda's two sisters and their husbands and children were leaving for California. A last-ditch effort to save the ranch by finding investors.

"Will I get to see the ocean?" Cody asked for the hundredth time. He'd never been anywhere but the ranch and was thrilled at the idea of traveling.

"Yes, honey. We'll make sure you get to see the ocean," Abby said. She looked at Belinda, her brow furrowed with worry. "Are you sure you don't want to come with us? I hate you being here all by yourself."

Belinda smiled. "I'm positive. And don't worry about me. I'm a big girl. Besides, I won't be by myself. The ranch hands will be here."

"Yes, but it still doesn't feel right going off and leaving you."

"Abby, it's the only way to do it. Somebody needs to stay and keep things running. Really, I don't mind," Belinda assured her.

"We should be back within ten days...two weeks tops," Luke said as he helped himself to a second stack of pancakes.

"It doesn't matter how long it takes if you get what we need," Belinda replied.

"I'd feel better about going off and leaving you here if Junior had been able to find out who forced you off the road last week," Colette interjected.

Belinda shrugged. "When I made the report, I didn't really expect Junior to be able to find out anything. I couldn't give him much information. I'm sure it was just some drunk. Anyway, my car is now fixed and I'll be just fine."

A knock on the back door interrupted their breakfast conversation. Belinda got up and answered, surprised to see Roger Eaton. The ranch hand stood, hat in hand, looking ill at ease as he shifted from foot to foot.

"'Morning, Belinda."

"Good morning, Roger. What's up?" It was rare for one of the hands to come to the house unless something was wrong.

"I was wondering if I could talk to you and your sisters about something...it's pretty important."

The early morning sun glinted off his blond hair and emphasized dark circles beneath his eyes. A sudden apprehension rippled through Belinda as she felt the tension that radiated from him.

"Come in. We were just having breakfast." Belinda opened the door to allow him entry into the large kitchen. "Would you like a cup of coffee?" She gestured to an empty chair near the table, but he shook his head and remained standing.

"No, thanks." Again he shifted from foot to foot as they all looked at him.

"I hope you aren't going to quit on me, Roger," Abby said. "I know things have been sort of rough around here lately, but you've been one of our best workers for the past couple of months."

"No...that's not why I'm here." He smoothed his thick, blond mustache with two fingers. "I guess there's no easy way to say this, so I'm just going to say it right out." He looked first at Abby, then at Colette, and finally at Belinda. "I'm here to find out which one of you is my half-sister."

There was a long moment of stunned silence. Belinda felt as if she'd been sucker punched by Roger's words. She suddenly remembered a moonlit night long ago when three little girls had pledged their sisterhood and agreed to never find out which of them might be adopted. As she looked at her sisters, she knew they were also remembering that distant night.

"I'm not sure I understand," Abby said. "You'd better sit down, Roger, and tell us what you're talking about."

Roger nodded and sat in the chair Belinda had indicated moments before. "My name isn't really Roger Eaton. It's Roger Whinnert. My father is James Whinnert." He paused a moment to allow that information to sink in. James Whinnert was a well-respected senator for the state of Montana.

He smoothed his mustache again, then reached into his back pocket and withdrew his wallet. He opened it and took out a driver's license and a newspaper clipping. He unfolded the clipping and handed it and the license to Belinda.

She took them from him, her mind whirling with questions and emotions too deep, too confused, to explore at the moment. The license showed his picture, along with the name Roger Whinnert. The newspaper article was brief, accompanied by a picture of the distinguished gray-haired senator and Roger. Taken at a charity ball, the caption read "Senator and son attend spring gala." Passing them to Colette, Belinda stared at Roger, somehow knowing in her heart he was about to rip apart the fabric of her family.

"My mother passed away soon after my birth and my father never remarried, but he did have a long relationship with a woman who lived in Washington, D.C. A year ago that woman died, but before she passed, she wrote my father a letter, telling him she'd given birth to his daughter years ago and that the young woman had been adopted. It wasn't until about five months ago when her estate was settled that a letter was found stating that the girl now lived on the Connor ranch in Wyoming." He paused, as if giving them a chance to digest each climactic morsel of his story.

"Cody, put your plate in the sink and wash your hands, then get upstairs and clean your room," Abby instructed her son, who seemed not to notice the drama unfolding before his mother and aunts.

When Cody had left the room, Abby looked at

Roger in confusion. "Your father didn't know this woman had been pregnant with his child?"

Roger shook his head. "Theirs was an odd relationship. Father saw her only when he was in Washington, D.C. Months would go by when they didn't see each other. He's not even sure exactly what year she gave birth."

Belinda wanted him to stop. She didn't want to hear any more. Change had always frightened her and she feared his words would forever change the relationship she had with her sisters. In the deepest part of her heart, she feared the one who didn't really belong was her.

"Why the subterfuge? Why come here as a worker and give a false name?" Abby asked.

Roger ducked his head, as if in embarrassment. "From the moment my father found out about having a daughter, he's been possessed with the need to find her. Unfortunately, the day after getting the letter detailing her location, he suffered a series of strokes and has been in and out of hospitals for the past several months. He hasn't been well enough to set the wheels in motion to find her. I took it upon myself to do that. I wanted to come out here and check out what kind of woman my sister might be. I figured my father would be better off not knowing if she were dead, or addicted to drugs, or something as equally appalling."

He paused a moment, his jaw clenched with tension. "My father has a certain image to uphold, and he's vulnerable not only to scandal, but to blackmail. I needed to find out more details before opening Pandora's box." The tension left his jaw. "But in the months I've been here, I know my father would be proud to call any one of the three of you daughter, and I'd be just as proud to be a brother to any one of you.'' He gazed at each one of them with eyes the color of Belinda's. "So, which one of you three is adopted?''

"We don't know,'' Colette answered after a moment's pause. "Abby found an envelope marked 'adoption papers' when we were young. We all agreed we wouldn't look at them. At that time we didn't want to know which one of us might be adopted.''

"But you have to look at them now.'' Roger sat forward on the chair, his jaw once again tightened with tension. "I got a phone call last night that my father has had another heart attack, this one worse than any he's had before. Time might be running out for him and his one wish is to meet his daughter.''

Belinda's heart convulsed with anxiety. She knew they'd do what he asked. They'd open the papers and discover which of them was his sister. A dying man's wish was more important than a childish vow made long ago.

"We have one small problem,'' Abby said. "I don't know where the papers are. When I went through Mother's and Father's things after their death, I didn't find those particular papers.''

"They've got to be around here someplace,'' Colette replied. She looked at Abby, then Belinda. "We'll just have to look until we find them.''

"I can't tell you what it would mean to my father,'' Roger replied as he stood. He looked at Abby. "If it's all right, I'd like a couple of days off. I want to fly home and check on my father.''

"Of course. Take as much time as you need," Abby replied.

"The last report I got was that he's stabilized, but I won't feel comfortable until I see him for myself. In the meantime, if you could find those papers...I'd love to be able to give my dad some answers as soon as possible.''

"We'll do our best to find answers for you," Abby said. The three sisters stood, as well, and for a moment there was an awkward silence. Belinda felt as if she should say something...do something. After all, Roger might possibly be her half-brother.

Roger seemed to sense their internal turmoil. "I don't expect anything around here to change. Until you find those papers and we know which of you is my sister, I intend to do my job just like all the other ranch hands." Without waiting for a reply, he nodded goodbye and left the house.

"I think I'll go check on some things in the barn," Luke said as he rose from the table.

"I'll go with you." Hank also stood. Belinda realized the two men were leaving to give the sisters some time alone to digest what they'd just heard.

"I always feared a day like this would come." Abby finally broke the silence as she sank down at the table.

"Nothing is going to change," Colette replied. "I don't care what those papers say, nothing is going to change the fact that you two are my sisters.''

"I agree," Abby echoed.

Belinda nodded, but her heart beat an uneasy

rhythm. Although she knew nothing could ever change the love she had for Abby and Colette, she knew nothing ever stayed static, and opening those adoption papers would change things between them. If what Roger said was true, one of them was the daughter of a U.S. senator.

"Do you think Roger was telling us the truth?" Colette asked, as if hearing Belinda's last thought.

Abby shrugged. "It sounded rather farfetched, but somehow had the ring of truth to it."

"He did have that newspaper clipping," Belinda reminded them.

Abby sighed, her face mirroring the expression of stun that Belinda knew her own features wore. "I know there are boxes of papers and pictures and such in the basement, and some things still in the closet in Mom and Dad's room. I've got a few things in the office I'll need to go through again. I don't know, maybe I overlooked the papers before."

"I'll go through the things in the basement," Belinda offered.

"And I'll search the bedroom and see what I can find," Colette said.

Without discussing it, Belinda realized they had come to the decision to rescind the vow they'd made so many years before. Silently the three began clearing the breakfast dishes from the table.

"NOTHING," Belinda said several hours later as she joined her sisters in the living room. "I found pictures, old report cards and handmade little gifts in those boxes in the basement. But no adoption papers."

"And I didn't find anything in the bedroom," Colette said.

Abby shook her head. "Nothing in the office, either. I think I'll go into town to see if I can speak with Mack Hargrove. As Mom and Dad's lawyer for so many years, maybe he'll know something about the papers."

"If you don't mind, I'll ride into town with you. I've been intending to pick up a couple of sweaters for Brook," Colette explained.

Abby nodded and looked at Belinda. "Want to take a ride with us?"

Belinda shook her head. "No, thanks. I think maybe I'll take Candy out for a ride."

"It's a gorgeous day for it," Abby observed.

Within minutes Abby, Colette, their husbands and kids had left for town. Belinda pulled on a lightweight jacket and stepped out onto the front porch.

The late afternoon sun was warm despite a slight nip in the air. The shadows cast by the trees and structures were long and deep, portending the coming sunset.

Billy Sims, one of the ranch hands, worked on a distant corral fence, painting a new section white to match the rest of the fencing. Belinda watched him for a moment. Abby had fired the sullen, dark-haired cowboy several months before because of his uncontrollable drinking problem. She'd recently rehired him, giving him a second chance at staying sober. It seemed all their workers had secrets, but none affected the Connor sisters as Roger's did.

She frowned, recreating Roger's features in her mind. Was it possible she was his sister? Did they share similar physical characteristics? They both had blue eyes, but so did Abby...as well as millions of other people in the world. Roger was fair, as was Belinda, but again that was no proof that they shared common genes.

She shook her head in an attempt to dispel those thoughts. Time would tell. When they found the adoption papers they would know which of them was Roger's sister. In the meantime, what she wanted most was to ride hard and fast, clear the muck from her mind.

Heading for the barn, she tried to dismiss all thoughts of Roger and the startling information he'd told her and her sisters.

She entered the barn and paused a moment for her eyes to adjust to the semidarkness. She heard a deep male voice coming from one of the stalls and recognized it as Bulldog's. She found him brushing down Blackheart, Abby's favorite horse. For a moment she stood just outside the stall door, listening to him coo and murmur to the horse.

"*C'est un jour parfait... Parfait...* That sounds like ice cream, don't it, Blackheart," he said.

Belinda froze. Bulldog was speaking French? As she remembered her parting words to Derek on the night of the Harvest Moon Dance, her blood boiled.

"Hi, Bulldog." She opened the stall door and stepped inside where the huge man worked on the black horse.

"Hey, Belinda." His eyes crinkled at the corners with his pleasure. "What are you doing out here?"

"I thought I'd take Candy for a ride," she explained.

He nodded. "It's a pretty evening for a nice ride." He placed the brush down and smiled at her again. *"C'est un jour parfait pour semarier."* He said the words slowly, carefully. "That's French." He beamed at her. "It means it's a perfect day to get married."

Don't shoot the messenger, Belinda thought to herself, knowing Bulldog had no idea the French message would needle her. "Let me guess. Derek taught you how to say that."

Bulldog nodded his head. "He surely did. Derek is my friend. He's helping me learn French so I can impress Rhonda. She knows how to talk French."

Again Belinda's blood flowed hot and angry. How dare he manipulate Bulldog just to get under her skin? Well, she'd just ride over to Derek's place and give him a piece of her mind. Saying goodbye to Bulldog, she headed for Candy's stall.

Within minutes she rode out of the corral on Candy. While Abby and Colette preferred more spirited, challenging mounts, Belinda's favorite was the gentle, sweet-natured quarterhorse with the caramel-colored mane.

She decided to ride for a while before heading to Derek's. She gave Candy free rein, allowing the horse to set their pace as they passed the corrals and outbuildings and headed for open pasture.

She passed the dragon tree, its branches ablaze with autumn colors and again she thought of the vow she and her sisters had made so long ago.

On that particular night they had been children and the idea that one of them might be adopted had frightened them all. They were no longer children, but Belinda was still frightened. She'd always gained her strength from her sisters, her family, and she didn't want anything to taint the very special relationship the three Connor women shared.

No matter how they all agreed that nothing would change, Belinda knew they were fooling themselves. Change was inevitable when the adoption papers were opened.

As Candy broke from a gallop to a run, Belinda threw her head back, wanting the brisk wind to blow her thoughts away as easily as it whipped her hair from the neat braid down her back.

She rode for a long time, letting the physical pleasure and rhythm of riding Candy soothe the tension that had knotted inside her for days.

Lately it seemed that each dawn brought a new set of problems rather than the promise of a beautiful day. The constant stress of trying to figure out how to save their home, Derek's unexpected return and crazy ideas for marriage and now Roger's bombshell...her nerves had been stretched taut for too long and she feared a snap was imminent.

The oranges and pinks of sunset faded from the sky as she turned Candy around and headed for the Walker place. Perhaps a little explosion of ire would be good for her soul, and she knew just who she wanted to aim a little ire toward.

She broke into the clearing of the Walker property and reined Candy to a halt, surprised at the house that seemed to have magically appeared since the last time she'd been here.

The former Walker house had been a simple one-story structure. The one that rose before her was two-story, with a wide, wrapping veranda that extended across the front and around to one side. Although unpainted and without trimwork, it was easy to visualize how attractive the house would be when completed.

"What do you think?" Derek's voice startled her, and she squinted her eyes to find him sitting in the shadows on the veranda.

"I'm impressed," she said reluctantly.

"Why don't you get down from that horse and let me give you the twenty-five-cent tour?" He stood and approached her.

Although touring his new home was not the reason she'd come, she found herself curious to see inside the place where Derek would more than likely live out the rest of his life. She dismounted and tied Candy to the porch railing, then followed Derek through the front door.

While the outside looked like a traditional two-story, the inside belied the exterior facade. Belinda caught her breath as she stepped into a huge room with floor-to-ceiling windows across the back wall. The space was big enough to be divided into a formal living room, family room and kitchen, but it was obvious Derek had opted to forgo walls and instead create one large and airy living area.

"This will be the heart of the house, where we'll eat our meals, talk about our day, watch the kids do their homework."

Belinda studiously ignored the subtle implication that somehow she would be a part of his future family life. She wasn't about to get caught up in any fantasy he might spin to trap her into agreeing to his preposterous marriage scheme.

"Come on upstairs and see the rest of the house."

Reluctantly she followed him up the wide oak stairway to the upper level. The first room he led her to was obviously the master suite. A cot covered with blankets held center court in the otherwise empty, unfinished room. "I'm spending nights out here," he explained. "I'm not taking any chances of somebody burning me out before I even get completely settled in."

"Have you had a chance to speak with Junior about the original fire?" Belinda asked, trying to keep her mind focused away from the huge Jacuzzi tub that was the focal point of one corner of the room. It was far too easy to imagine the room lit with candles, bubbles spilling out as Derek folded his lanky length to join her in a tub of sweet-scented water.

He nodded, his eyes dark and hooded, giving nothing away of his inner thoughts. "I got copies of the reports a couple of days ago. Unfortunately there isn't much to go on. All we really know is the fire started in the hallway just outside my bedroom and it was started with gasoline. A gas can was found in the woods, but there were no fingerprints on it."

"How would somebody have gotten into the hallway?" she asked.

He shrugged. "I'd left the front door unlocked, knowing that Mom and Dad might come in early in the morning. I never worried about locking the doors at night. This was my home, my community, and I trusted in its safety." The blankness in his eyes dissipated, overshadowed by a cool hardness. "I won't make the same mistake twice. Now I trust nobody."

Yes, that's what Belinda saw in his eyes. A loss of

innocence. A naiveté betrayed. She recognized it because she'd lost the same when she'd received his letter after the fire. Innocence lost and illusions destroyed.

"This will be Tasha's room," he said as he led her into one of the rooms on the opposite side of the staircase from the master suite. "She's the five-year-old. You'll like her, she's so bright and loving."

"And this will be Toby's room," Derek explained as they entered another room. His features softened into a half smile. "Toby has been lost since his parents' accident. He's become pretty withdrawn. He's going to require lots of love and attention."

Belinda didn't want to hear about these children. Already with just his brief description of the two parentless kids her heart swelled with compassion. And memories of another child.

She walked back down the stairway, wanting out of this house he was building, away from the future he was carefully planning for himself and the two children. "It's a wonderful house," she said as she reached the front door. "And you should be very happy here."

He leaned against the stair railing, his eyes once again cold and distant. "I don't think about my own happiness much."

His words created a haunting inside Belinda. What had happened to him in the last three years that had made him change? She knew why she'd lost her ability to dream of happiness, but what had happened to him?

Her very curiosity about him irritated her. He was the past, her past, and she had no desire to revisit that past in any way. "Derek, I came by because I want you to leave Bulldog alone. I don't like the idea of you manipulating a friendship with him just to teach him a little French and get under my skin."

"I'm not manipulating a friendship with Bulldog. He is a friend." A small smile curved the corners of his mouth. "And he shows a real aptitude for foreign languages."

Belinda opened the door and stepped out onto the porch, surprised that while they'd been inside the sun had gone down, leaving the surreal illumination of twilight.

"Belinda." Derek grabbed her arm before she could step off the porch. He pulled her up against him, his closeness stealing her breath away. "All I'm asking from you is a little bit of your time." The warmth of his breath fanned her face and the scent of him surrounded her. Heat radiated from his body, a warmth that counteracted the coolness of the night air.

She struggled to step away from him. "Let me go."

"Not until you've heard everything I have to say."

He sighed, but didn't release his hold on her. "I'll admit I was wrong to tell the judge my marriage to you was imminent. But I wanted those kids and your name popped into my head before I'd consciously thought everything through." He let go of her and stepped back, then raked a hand through his hair. "I've already promised you that the marriage would be in name only. I don't want a physical relationship with you, nor do I want any kind of emotional commitment. We had our time together years ago and that book is now closed. But, Belinda, I need you. Every day you procrastinate about our marriage is another day those two little kids stay in foster care.''

''That's not fair,'' she said angrily, hating his attempt to use the children to manipulate her into agreeing to his crazy plan. More, she was angry that he could so easily dismiss what they had once shared, insist he wanted nothing to do with her physically or emotionally. ''I've got to get back home before it gets dark.'' She untied Candy from the railing and mounted the horse.

''Belinda, we could both gain from the marriage. I'm not making you a one-sided offer. I can relieve the financial pressures you and your sisters have been under.''

''Colette and Abby and my brothers-in-law are taking off for California first thing in the morning to speak with prospective investors. I'm sure our financial worries will be over within the next week or two.'' She picked up the reins to urge Candy away, but hesitated as Derek spoke her name again.

''Please.''

The word fell from his lips as if pulled by great force, and Belinda knew how difficult it was for him to say. Derek was a proud and stubborn man, and she used to tease him because of his reluctance to say that particular word. ''Saying please feels too much like begging,'' he used to protest. ''And there's nothing so important that it would make me beg.''

Now he'd said it and Belinda's heart constricted as she saw the fervent emotion shimmering in his eyes, letting her know just how important those children were to him.

She admired him caring for them...and hated him

for it at the same time. That he would go to such extremes for his niece and nephew, yet had virtually turned his back on his own child, made her heart ache with a renewed force. "I've got to get home." Flicking the reins, she nodded goodbye, then turned Candy around to begin the ride back to her ranch.

Candy had taken only a step or two when a loud report split the surrounding silence. Candy's ears folded back and her eyes rolled as she skittered sideways in nervous high-steps. As Belinda fought to keep control of the horse, Derek looked out into the distance, obviously trying to discern where the shot might have come from.

"You see anyone?" Belinda asked, finally managing to calm Candy.

He shook his head. "I'm not even sure what direction it came from. Probably a hunter who doesn't realize this is private property."

Before Belinda had a chance to reply, another blast resounded and she heard the whistle of a bullet whiz by her head. Candy reared up on hind legs. A terrified whinny tore from the horse's throat as she bucked Belinda off her back.

Belinda fell to the ground with a thud, all breath leaving her body.

"Belinda!" Derek shouted from the porch.

Vaguely aware of the sound of Candy's hooves as the horse raced off, Belinda drew in a gasping breath and tried to stand. "I'm okay," she said as she finally got to her feet.

Again the sharp crack of gunfire rent the air and Derek dove into her, tackling her back to the ground. For the first time confusion gave way to fear as she felt Derek's heart racing against her own. "What's happening?" she asked, body tense as she waited for whatever might happen next.

Derek remained on top of her—the only thing moving were his eyes as they scanned the thickly wooded area in the distance.

He glanced down at her, his eyes dark and disturbed. "It appears whoever is hunting…is hunting us."

Chapter Five

"Can you see anything?" Belinda asked softly.

"No." Derek continued to scan the area, his muscles tensed as he tried to see somebody—anybody—in the nearby woods.

There was no doubt in his mind that whoever had fired the gun had fired it at them. The first shot could have been written off as an accident, an overzealous hunter who hadn't realized they were in the line of fire. The subsequent shots couldn't be mistaken for anything but a deliberate attack. Dammit, he should have been prepared for something like this. He should have been more cautious.

Belinda squirmed beneath him. "Stay still," he said sharply.

"There's a rock in my back," she whispered, her breath a warm sweetness against the hollow of his throat.

He reached beneath her, trying to ignore the thrust of her body against his as she arched to allow him access to the rock. He grabbed the offending object and removed it from beneath her. She sank against the ground.

Derek threw the rock into the tall grass to the right of them, tensing for the expected gunshot blast the noise might draw. Nothing. No shot. Nothing at all.

Seconds turned into minutes as Derek remained tensed, watchful. Each moment brought a deepening of the night, cloaking them in the safety of darkness. As the minutes stretched, he became conscious of the sweet scent of wildflowers nearby and the beat of Belinda's heart against his own.

Desire came as unexpectedly as the shots had and struck him hard in the pit of his stomach. It surprised him. He'd thought all capability for desire had burned up in the flames that had left him half crippled.

Bitterness clogged the back of his throat. He could desire, but he'd never again be desirable. Anger usurped desire, an anger directed at Belinda, who unwittingly could still stir his blood with lust.

He rose hesitantly, instinctively knowing the shooter had gone. A bird cried from a nearby tree and the clicking and buzzing of night insects filled the air. "I think it's okay now."

"Are you sure?" She remained on her back, the moonlight illuminating her features and painting her hair with incandescent strands. With the dark grass beneath her, and her blue eyes shimmering almost silver, she looked much the way she had years ago when Derek had made love to her beneath a full summer moon.

Again anger surfaced as memories whispered in his head, taunting him with what might have been, what would now never be. "I'm positive." He stood and eyed the dark woods from where the shots had come. "Whoever was there, isn't there any longer."

Belinda rose and brushed off the seat of her slacks, her gaze following his. "Who on earth would do such a thing?"

"Who knows? We need to call Junior and report this. Come on back in the house. I've got a phone inside." Belinda remained downstairs in the foyer while he went up to the bedroom where he'd been staying. It took only moments for him to call the sheriff, then he and Belinda sat on the front porch to await Junior's arrival.

"You want me to see if I can find your horse?" he asked, biding time so he could think, assess the mounting danger surrounding Belinda.

She shook her head. "I'm sure she went back to the stable. She has good instincts for home." She wrapped her arms around her shoulders, as if chilled. Derek suspected it was fear rather than the coolness of the night air that chilled her. "Why on earth would somebody want to shoot at you?" she asked as she leaned back against the porch railing.

"I was just about to ask you the same thing."

Her eyes widened in surprise. "Surely you don't believe those bullets were meant for me?"

Derek frowned, replaying the initial moments of the first shot in his mind. "I'm not sure what to believe. All I know is when the first shot came, you were some distance from where I stood, and that bullet nearly hit you. As did the second one. If the shooter was after me, then we're dealing with a hunter with a very bad aim."

"But why would anyone want to harm me?" Belinda shook her head thoughtfully. "It doesn't make any sense that somebody is after me." She shook her head more vehemently. "No. Somehow this has to be tied to you."

Derek knew better. If she gave it enough thought, she'd realize it seemed farfetched to believe that a fire three years ago and a shooting now might be related. Although he wanted to find the person who'd hated him enough to try to kill him before, it was far more important he figure out who wanted to harm Belinda.

Looking at her, he noted again how the moonlight loved her features, caressing her in a silvery light that only intensified her natural beauty.

Had he been smart, he'd never have come back here where thoughts of her could torment him. He'd have gone to another city, another state, and tried his damnedest to put her out of his mind forever.

But he'd been drawn back here by memories, trapped in the lies he'd blurted to a judge, caught in a web of threats sent to him by an unknown antagonist.

The fact that somebody had tried to kill him three years ago concerned him. The fact that somebody wanted to hurt Belinda infuriated him.

"Did Junior ever find out who forced you off the road the night of the Harvest Moon Dance?" he asked.

Again her eyes flickered with surprise. "No. Why? Do you think that has something to do with tonight?"

He shrugged and released a deep sigh. "I'm just trying to make some sort of sense out of the senseless."

"I don't think that my getting forced off the road has anything to do with this. Junior believes whoever was responsible for that was probably just drunk and careless. I think he's right.'' She leaned her head forward and closed her eyes. As Derek watched, she rubbed her forehead, as if trying to ease an ache deep inside her head.

"Headache?" he asked.

"I feel like my brain is about to explode from overload." She looked at Derek, her eyes darkened by confusion. "First there's the worry about hanging on to the ranch."

"Which you can fix by saying two little words to me," he reminded her. "I do. That's all it will take."

She frowned her displeasure at his interruption. "As if that's not enough," she continued, "one of our ranch hands informed us this morning that he's certain one of us is his long-lost sister."

Derek stared at her in shock. "What?"

As Belinda explained about the adoption papers found long ago, and Roger Eaton's claim of family, Derek realized again that the relationship he'd thought he and Belinda had shared three years before had been little more than a surface one.

He'd believed she'd shared everything with him, told him all the secrets contained in her soul, but he now recognized that she'd held private areas of her heart that she'd never allowed him to enter. No wonder she hadn't tried too hard to maintain their love. She'd never really given him her heart. "You never told me you might be adopted," he said.

Before she could answer, Junior's car pulled into view. Derek stood, shoving thoughts of the past away. He needed Belinda, but he'd never make the mistake of loving her again. And if she hadn't been able to love him years ago when he'd been a whole man, she certainly wouldn't fall in love with him now, scarred and bitter.

As Junior got out of his car, Belinda stood and together she and Derek went out to meet the sheriff. "Evening," the lawman said as they approached. "What's going on?"

"That's what we'd like to know," Belinda said. As she explained to Junior what had happened, Derek once again perused the dark wooded area from where he thought the shots had come.

"You don't think it was some kind of an accident?" Junior asked.

Derek shook his head. "I might have been able to dismiss it all as an accident if there'd only been one shot. But there were several and there's no way in hell it wasn't deliberate."

Junior leaned into his car and grabbed a flashlight from the front seat. "Guess I'll have a look around."

"I'll go with you," Derek said.

"I'll just wait up on the porch," Belinda added, sounding weary and still a little shaken by the entire incident.

"I don't think those shots were intended for me," Derek said to Junior as the two men began walking toward the woods.

Junior eyed him sharply. "You think somebody was trying to harm Belinda?"

Derek shrugged. "The first two shots seemed directed entirely toward her."

"I hope you're wrong about that," Junior replied with a heavy sigh. "Those Connor girls have seen more than their share of trouble over the last couple of months. I'd like to think the bad times are all behind them now.''

Junior shone the flashlight toward the grove of trees just ahead of them. ''You think the shots came from someplace around there?''

''With the echo effect, it's difficult to say exactly where they came from,'' Derek explained, ''but this is the only viable place for somebody to hide, so they had to come from here.''

Together the two men followed the illumination of the flashlight, attempting to locate where a gunman might have stood or any other clues to help answer who and why.

Fallen leaves littered the ground, crunching noisily beneath their feet as they searched the area. As the sheriff's light swept back and forth, Derek caught a glimpse of something gleaming amid the leaves.

''Hold it,'' he said. ''Back here.'' He indicated for Junior to shine the light in the area he'd just passed. Derek bent and picked up a gleaming gold shotgun shell. ''Bingo,'' he said softly, and held the shell out to Junior.

''A twelve gauge,'' Junior observed. ''Somebody meant business.''

Derek continued to pick through the leaves and came up with two more shells. He straightened and looked toward the house. With the light of the moon spilling down, he could easily see the front porch and the place where Belinda had mounted her horse. ''Whoever it was, they stood here and fired.'' The shells felt heavy in his hand. ''There's no way it was an accident. There's nothing impeding the view from here.''

A chill danced up Derek's spine as he thought of somebody crouched here in the cover of the woods, watching him and Belinda, then carefully taking aim and squeezing the trigger.

"You sure they were aiming at Belinda and not you?" Junior asked.

Derek hesitated before answering. It was time to tell somebody what had brought him back here, time to trust somebody. "Yeah, I'm pretty sure," he finally replied. "About a month ago I started getting notes telling me Belinda was in danger." Junior stared at him in surprise. "That's part of what brought me back here. I want her protected."

Junior frowned, looking old and tired in the pale moonlight. "What, exactly, did these notes say?"

Derek leaned against a tree trunk and rubbed his thigh thoughtfully. "That she was going to die, that she had to die."

Junior sucked in a long breath, then released it slowly. "And you don't know who might have sent those notes?"

Derek shook his head. "Not a clue. They were block-lettered on plain paper and postmarked from here."

"Why would this person write to you?"

"I don't know," Derek replied, although he assumed it had been a ploy to get him back to town. Somebody knew how deeply he'd once felt about Belinda and was now using those emotions to bring him back here. But why?

"You have those notes?" Junior asked.

"Inside the house."

"I'd like to see them."

Derek nodded and pushed off from the tree. "I'll bring them by your office first thing in the morning. At the moment I'd prefer Belinda not know about them. Can you provide some kind of protection for her?"

Junior's frown deepened, causing the lines and wrinkles in his tanned skin to intensify. "Derek, there's no way I can do that. I'm working without a deputy right now and even hiring a dozen more men, we'd all be overworked."

"Couldn't the Cheyenne police department loan you a couple of men?"

"For what? Right now all I've got is some anonymous notes and what might be construed as a random shooting." Junior sighed. "There's no point in us fumbling around out here in the dark," he said. "I'll come back out early in the morning and take a look around, see if there's anything else to find."

Derek nodded. Just as he suspected, he was the only protection Belinda would get. If she was going to stay safe, it would be up to him. He and Junior started back toward the house.

"You think it wise to keep those notes from her?"

"Hell, I don't know what's wise and what isn't. Initially I didn't want to frighten her. I didn't know if the notes were somebody's idea of a sick joke or what." He stopped walking and turned to Junior. "The other reason why I haven't said anything to her is that there's a possibility she isn't the target at all. Somebody wanted me back here, and it's possible Belinda is merely the bait."

"You think this has something to do with the fire at your place?"

"I don't know." Derek looked toward the porch, where Belinda's silhouette was visible against the light wood of the house. "The fire was a long time ago. Hard for me to believe this is all tied together. All I know is that I intend to make sure nobody gets to me, and I'm sure as hell not going to let anyone get to Belinda."

As they reached the porch, Belinda stood. "Did you find anything?"

"Shells," Derek answered.

"Unfortunately they won't do us any good unless we have a gun to check them against. And half the ranchers in the state have twelve-gauge shotguns," Junior replied.

Derek nodded absently, his gaze lingering on Belinda. Who could possibly want to harm her? Why would anyone want to? Was the car that forced her off the road a week earlier really a drunk? Or was this all a sick game to get to him?

"No point in me hanging around any longer," Junior said, breaking into Derek's thoughts. "I'll be out here at first light to check the area a little more thoroughly."

"Junior, would you mind dropping me home?" Belinda asked the lawman.

"I'll take you home," Derek replied.

Her eyes flashed with some emotion Derek couldn't decipher. Something deeper than fear and yet he couldn't imagine why she'd be afraid of him. It was there only a moment then gone. "Thanks, but I'll just catch a ride with Junior," she replied.

With a curt nod, Derek watched as Junior and Belinda got into the patrol car. Gravel crunched and spit beneath the tires as the car pulled away. Derek sank down onto the porch, his thoughts once again in chaos.

Was it possible the attack tonight had been aimed at him? Was it possible that whatever hatred had burned down his house and nearly killed him three years before had been festering...waiting for his return?

If the attack had not been aimed at him, and rather at Belinda, then what could she possibly have done to garner such malevolence? And who had sent him those notes? Somebody trying to warn him...or somebody attempting to lure him?

"YOU ALL RIGHT?" Junior asked as they pulled away from Derek's house.

"A little shaken up, but I'm fine." It was a lie. She wasn't fine and she was more than just a little shaken. What bothered her was that she didn't know which had frightened her more: the bullets coming from an unknown assailant or the force of her physical reaction when Derek had been on top of her.

A bullet might provide a quick, merciful death. Caring about Derek in any way, shape or form would be a slow, painful kind of death.

"So, have you tangled with anyone lately? Made somebody mad at you?" Junior's question interrupted her thoughts.

"No." She flashed him a quick smile. "You know me, Junior. I'm fairly nonconfrontational. It comes from being the middle child between two dynamos like Abby and Colette."

Junior offered her a wry grin. "Those two do tend

to be bullheaded…and don't you go telling them I said that.''

Belinda smiled at the gray-haired old man, affection welling up in her heart. Since their father's death, Junior had become a surrogate father, checking in on them often, offering his support and wisdom.

''Junior, you were best friends with Dad. Did he ever tell you one of us was adopted?''

Junior shot her a look of surprise and shook his head slowly. ''No, honey, he never mentioned it. Of course, the three of you girls were just tiny things when your daddy bought the ranch and moved here. If one of you was adopted, it didn't matter to him. I've never seen a man who loved his girls like your daddy did. Your mama was the same way, devoted to you girls.''

Belinda nodded, a knot of grief clogging her throat as she thought of her parents, now gone for more than six years.

''Want to tell me what's going on?'' Junior asked.

Swallowing hard against the grief, Belinda explained to the sheriff about Roger's claim. ''I can't imagine why Roger would lie about all this. He has nothing to gain by claiming any familial ties.'' She laughed, the sound hollow. ''It's not like he can possibly be after our money. We don't have any.''

''I still don't like the sound of it. I'm going to check out this Roger Eaton…or Roger Whinnert, and see what I can come up with,'' Junior said as he pulled up in front of the Connor house.

''And you'll let us know what you find out?''

''Of course I will.'' He put the car in park and turned to Belinda, his features appearing old and tired in the glow from the dashboard. "I let you girls down before. I won't do it again."

Belinda reached over and covered his hand with hers, knowing he still felt guilty because he hadn't suspected his deputy was working with their foreman to try to get their ranch. "You couldn't have known about Richard Helstrom. He fooled us all."

"But I should have known. It's my job." He cleared his throat and gave her hand a squeeze. "If there are skeletons in this Roger Eaton's closet, I'll find them. If there's even a hint of something not right with his story, I'll let you know."

She nodded and opened her car door to get out.

"Belinda?"

She hesitated and looked back at him.

"I heard the rest of the family is leaving in the morning to go to California."

"That's right. We're hoping to find some investors."

"Maybe you should go stay with a friend or something. I don't like the idea of you being out here all by yourself." His forehead puckered with a frown. "You've had two close calls in the last couple of weeks."

Belinda gazed at him quizzically, then realized what he was talking about. "I can't imagine that the car running me off the road has anything to do with what happened tonight," she protested. She smiled reassuringly at the old man. "Don't worry. I'll be fine. I can't imagine why anyone would be after me. And as far as the incident tonight goes, I think you'd better ask Derek who he's tangled with since returning to town. Maybe whoever tried to burn down his house three years ago isn't too happy to see him back in town."

"Maybe," Junior agreed thoughtfully. "But until we know who was responsible for the shots tonight, until we know why, I want you to be especially cautious."

"I will. I promise." With a final goodbye, Belinda got out of the car and watched as it pulled back down the road, the taillights finally disappearing into the darkness of the night.

Wrapping her arms around herself, she stood for a moment, allowing the sounds to soothe her frayed nerves. Out here, with the moon shining down and the night creatures clicking and singing their lullabies, it was hard to take Junior's warning too seriously.

A soft whinny from the corral outside the barn reminded Belinda about Candy. Belinda headed in that direction.

As she passed the bunkhouse, she noticed it was dark and quiet. During the week the ranch hands usually bedded down early. She checked her watch, surprised to realize it was nearly ten o'clock. Not only was the bunkhouse dark and silent, but so was the main house. Everyone there had probably gone to bed early in preparation for their trip in the morning.

Candy greeted her, nuzzling her hand as Belinda stepped into the corral. "Hi, girl. You found your way home, huh." Belinda stroked the horse behind the ears for a moment, then opened the barn door. She led Candy inside, pausing to turn on the bare light that dangled on a long wire from the ceiling.

She unsaddled Candy, then led the horse back to her stall. The light barely penetrated the dark shadows in this area of the barn. But Belinda was as familiar with this area as she was with her own bedroom.

"Here you go, girl," she murmured softly as she moved the horse into the wooden confines. Fresh hay had been placed on the floor and smelled sweet and clean. Knowing she should go to bed, but too wound up for sleep, Belinda grabbed a curry brush and began to work down Candy's flanks.

The horse stood patiently, apparently enjoying the touch of the brush against her sides and back. As Belinda worked, her mind raced with everything that had happened at Derek's.

Oh, why, when she was around him did she find it so hard to reach within herself and find the hate she wanted to feel for him? What magic did he spin that made her still weak and breathless at his mere touch?

She froze. She thought she heard something, something like the soft pad of footsteps on hay. Candy raised her head and sniffed the air, as if sensing something amiss.

Belinda set the brush down and carefully opened the stall door, frowning as it creaked on rusty hinges. "Hello?" she called hesitantly. "Is anyone there?"

Silence. Utter silence. Candy nervously pawed the straw beneath her hooves and snorted as if trying to tell Belinda something.

As Belinda remembered that moment of sitting astride Candy and the whiz of the bullet by her head, cold chills shivered up her spine. Had somebody tried to shoot her at Derek's and when that had failed, followed her here?

As long as she remained in Candy's stall she was trapped, an easy victim for whoever might be out there. Breathing shallowly through her mouth, she moved out of the stall and toward the main area of the barn where the light shone more brightly.

She took several steps, then paused to listen. Again she heard the faint rustle of stealthy movement. Belinda's heart leapt into her throat as fear rippled through her. Somebody was definitely in the barn with her. The fact that whomever it was hadn't answered her call only made her fear intensify.

She'd been foolish to enter the barn alone at night while the rest of her family all slept. She'd told Junior she'd be cautious, then had proceeded to do something stupid.

Looking around for anything that could be used as a weapon, she tried to still the frantic pounding of her heart. A pitchfork leaned against the wall and she grabbed it, reassured by the wooden handle and sharp tines.

She advanced to where the light shone brightly, illuminating the entire area. "Is somebody here?" she asked, then stood still and listened.

Nothing. No answer, no sound at all. Seconds stretched into minutes and still Belinda didn't move. As she looked around, she began to feel foolish. Nothing appeared disturbed, nothing seemed amiss.

Leaning the pitchfork against a wall, she chided herself for overworking paranoia. She'd probably heard one of the barn cats that wandered in and out chasing mice.

With a final look around, she pulled the light chain, then left the barn, closing the door behind her. She turned and screamed as she encountered a solid body and hands gripped her shoulders.

"Billy!" She stepped back from the menacing, sullen-featured ranch hand. "What are you doing out here?"

He shoved his hands into his pockets, his dark eyes gleaming in the pale glow from the moon. "I saw the light in the barn and thought I'd better check it out."

"Were you inside the barn just now?" Belinda asked.

Billy shook his head, his dark, straight hair swinging around his narrow face. "I didn't get that far before you came out."

Belinda wasn't sure if she believed him or not, but she was definitely uncomfortable standing in the dark of night with him. "Everything is fine. You can go on back to the bunkhouse," she said.

She watched as he nodded curtly, then headed back in the direction from where he'd presumably come. Billy Sims. Had he lied to her? Had he been in the barn, waiting for the opportunity to harm her in some way?

Disturbing thoughts tumbled around in her head as she went into the house and carefully locked the door behind her. Once in her bedroom, she turned on the small lamp by the bed and changed into her nightgown.

Instead of getting directly into bed, she turned off the lamp and moved to the window, her mind still whirling in contemplation.

In the past several months her sisters had been plagued with strange "accidents." First, Colette had sworn she'd been pushed off the edge of a butte, then locked in the cellar at the Walker place. Then Abby had been hit with a hay bale tumbling from the loft in the barn. All three incidents had nearly deadly consequences and hadn't been fully explained to anyone's satisfaction. Was somebody playing deadly games with them?

She frowned, thinking of Billy Sims. She'd heard that Billy had lost visitation rights to his children after Abby had fired him. Was it possible he thought he had a grudge to settle with the Connors?

Rubbing her forehead, she turned away from the window and got into bed. She didn't know what to think. Perhaps the light of day would bring answers. She shivered, the dawn suddenly much too far away.

Chapter Six

"Drive safely," Belinda yelled, then waved to the occupants of the car that pulled down the driveway. She watched her family disappear from view, then hugged herself to ward off a sudden chill.

Early morning sunshine peeked out from behind the last of the night clouds, casting a golden glow to the landscape. The air was pungent with autumn scents and Belinda felt a sharp pierce of bereavement as she tried to imagine life any place else but here.

She'd tried to make a life for herself separate from the ranch when she'd moved to Kansas City. She'd been miserable. She knew so much of her and her sisters' strength came from the rugged terrain that made up this place of their roots.

Somehow, some way, Abby and Colette had to succeed in finding investors. They couldn't lose this place. They just couldn't.

Derek's proposal taunted her; a way to keep the ranch, a way to make her sisters happy. And yet Derek had made it clear he wanted no emotional entanglement. What he offered her had nothing to do with love, nothing to do with lifetime commitment. He needed a temporary wife and nothing more.

"Mornin', Belinda."

Belinda jumped at the sound of the deep voice behind her. She turned and smiled at Bulldog. "Good morning, Bulldog. You're up early."

He shrugged. "The sun's up, so I'm up." He looked in the direction where the Connor car had disappeared. "Looks like you're gonna be all alone for a while."

Belinda nodded. "For a couple of weeks."

"Aren't you scared of being alone?"

Belinda smiled at the big, childlike man. "Not really. I've got nothing to be afraid of in my own home."

Bulldog's broad forehead wrinkled with a deep frown. "I'm scared what's going to happen to me if you all sell the ranch." For a moment his features darkened with anger. "Your daddy always promised me I'd have a home here. If you sell, I don't know what I'll do."

"Bulldog, no matter what happens, we'll make sure you have a place to live, a place where you're happy." Belinda tried to reassure him.

"I'm happy here," he answered succinctly.

"So am I." For a moment the two of them stood silent in the dawn light, gazing at the land around them.

For the first time Belinda realized that in selling the ranch they were not only displacing themselves, but all the men who worked for them, as well. "Maybe whoever buys the ranch will let you stay on and you won't have to leave," she finally offered.

Bulldog's frown didn't ease. "I can't talk about it no more. It makes me too sad…and too mad." Without waiting for her reply, he turned and walked toward the barn.

Belinda watched him go, her heart aching with his fears of losing his home. The same fears that ached in her own heart.

She started to go into the house, then changed her mind and instead headed for the dragon tree. Throughout her life, anytime she'd been lonely, frightened or upset, sitting beneath the dragon tree had always brought her solace.

The leaves were at autumn peak, a fiery red that heightened the impression of a dragon breathing fire. Within days, the leaves would fall to the ground and the dragon would disappear until spring foliage once again created the form of the mythical beast.

She sank down at the base of the tree, studiously keeping her gaze from the direction where she knew she'd be able to see the roof of Derek's new house.

She didn't want to think about him, didn't want to analyze why she'd responded so passionately to his nearness when they'd been on the ground together the night before.

Instead, she closed her eyes and focused on just breathing in the sweet-scented morning air and clearing her mind of turmoil.

Within minutes she was asleep and dreaming. She knew it was a dream and fought against it as the vision of her and Derek making love unfolded in her mind.

The image filled her with wistful longing as she remembered the strength of his arms surrounding her, the heat of his kisses, the utter splendor of being loved by him.

The scene unfolded like a movie projected on the screen of her mind, and she watched in horror as flames began to consume the grass surrounding where they lay.

As the fire edged closer, the heat grew so intense it stole her breath. She struggled to escape, but Derek's arms tightened around her, holding her prisoner to his passion...and the flames.

"Good morning, Belinda."

She awoke with a start and snapped her eyes open to see Derek standing next to where she sat. Disoriented, she blinked several times in an effort to leave her dreams and reclaim reality.

"You're up early," he said as he sank down next to her in the cool grass. He took off his dusty brown hat and placed it beside him on the ground.

"The rest of my family left this morning for California. I got up to see them off, then came up here and promptly fell asleep and started dreaming."

"I hope I didn't interrupt pleasant dreams."

She pulled her knees up to her chest and wrapped her arms around them. "No, I'm grateful for the interruption. I was having a nightmare."

"Want to tell me about it?"

She shook her head as she felt a blush warm her face. "No, it's not important." Gazing at him, she noted how the early morning sunshine peeking through the tree leaves glinted on his blond hair and painted his face in warm hues. He looked like the handsome, golden cowboy of her past...of her dreams. She averted her gaze. "You're up and around early, too."

"Bear's crew is working every day from dawn until dusk. I got roused out of the house early for the men doing the interior painting."

"The house has gone up so quickly. They've probably set some kind of new world record," Belinda observed, wishing he didn't smell like sunshine and fresh rain and a subtle hint of spicy cologne.

He smiled, his eyes the warm brown she remembered so well. "It's amazing how quickly things can get accomplished when you're paying top dollar." He leaned against the tree trunk, his gaze lingering on her. "I wasn't surprised to find you here. You have always loved this tree."

"Yes." Belinda leaned back once again and straightened her legs out in front of her. "Mama loved this tree, and taught the three of us to love it, as well. Our dragon tree. She always talked like it was more than just a piece of wood, like it was some sort of guardian that could hear secrets and never tell, that listened to weaknesses and never judged."

She laughed softly. "I know it sounds crazy, but I always felt like this tree had all the wisdom, all the answers to all my problems, if I'd just learn to listen to what it had to say." A blush once again warmed her cheeks. "Pretty silly, huh."

He touched one of her hands, his fingers calloused, but not unpleasantly rough. "Not silly at all. I feel the same way about this land. That's part of what brought me back here."

She wanted to take her hand away from his, found

his touch too evocative, and yet didn't move to break the contact.

From the moment she'd heard he'd returned to town, she realized she'd been waiting for him to touch her, to attempt to rekindle the flames of desire that had burned so brightly between them years before.

She closed her eyes, wishing herself back in time when life was less complicated and there were no ghosts to haunt her happiness. A time when she'd loved Derek with no reservation, with a pure, unconditional love.

She suppressed a shiver as his touch moved from the back of her hand to the side of her face. She knew she should stop him, that she shouldn't allow him to touch her with the intimacy of a lover. But she didn't want to fight the sweet swell of passion that welled up inside her. It had been so long. Too long.

Opening her eyes, she gazed at him and saw her desire reflected in the brown depths of his eyes. His fingertips traced down the length of her jaw, then up to the outline of her lips.

"I didn't think it was possible that you could grow more beautiful, but you have," he said, his voice deep and husky.

She knew he was about to kiss her, and she did nothing to stop him. Rather she leaned forward, subtly encouraging him to claim her mouth with his. And he did. Tentative at first, then he deepened the kiss with a thrust of his tongue.

Immediately Belinda was cast into the past, to that time when her love for Derek had known no boundaries. She wrapped her arms around his neck, wanting the kiss to last forever. With his lips on hers, the heartaches of the past disappeared and the worries of the future fell away. There was only this moment and this man.

The kiss seemed to linger forever yet still be too brief. With a swiftness that stole her breath away, he released her and stood. With his back to her, he looked stiff and unyielding, his posture rigid as if in anger.

"Was it all lies, Derek?" she asked softly. "Everything we shared three years ago?"

He turned around to face her, his eyes dark and unfathomable. "No, it wasn't lies. It was childish dreams. But we aren't children any longer."

His words stirred her bitterness, the bitterness that was never far from the surface. Her love for him had been a woman's love and the knowledge that he could dismiss it as part of childhood ached in her heart. "Then why did you just kiss me?"

He smiled, a gesture that curved his lips but didn't touch the darkness of his eyes. "Because I wanted to, and you looked like you wanted it, too. Consider it a momentary regression."

"I'll simply consider it a mistake." She stood, the cold morning air suddenly chilling her throughout. "The day's a'wasting. I'd better get back."

She was grateful he said no more, but felt his gaze lingering on her as she walked away. She didn't stop walking until she was back on her porch.

Leaning on the railing, she replayed that moment of his kiss in her mind. How easily his kiss had cast her back in time, making her momentarily forget his betrayal, the ache of loss, the pain of a breaking heart.

But she could never forget or forgive how easily he'd walked out of her life before.

Unwilling to continue entertaining thoughts of Derek, she went inside and grabbed her purse and car keys. She'd surprise Janice and take her to breakfast. She'd hardly talked to her friend since the night of the Harvest Moon Dance.

It was a twenty-minute drive into the heart of Cheyenne where Janice had an apartment in a small but attractive complex.

Belinda wasn't surprised when Janice answered her knock still in her nightgown. Janice wasn't an early riser, and it was only a little after seven-thirty.

"Belinda...what are you doing here so early?" Janice raked a hand through her hair and gestured Belinda inside. She flopped down onto the sofa and Belinda sat on a chair across from her.

"I came to take you to breakfast. Wow, what happened to your shoulder?" Under the spaghetti strap of her pale pink nightgown, a vivid bruise darkened the skin of her upper shoulder.

"Oh, it's nothing. Stupid me walked into the bathroom door in the middle of the night." She stood. "If you'll wait just a minute, I'll throw some clothes on." She flashed Belinda a quick grin. "If I'm going to be awake this early, I might as well have breakfast." She disappeared into her bedroom.

Belinda got up and wandered around the neat living room, admiring Janice's decorative flair. There had been a time when Belinda couldn't wait to have her own place, space not shared by her two sisters.

Despite the painful events that had driven her out of her family home to Kansas City, she'd been excited about the prospect of living on her own. It hadn't taken long for that excitement to wan beneath the reality of a dingy studio apartment, a waitressing job, and a burgeoning pregnancy. She'd been thrilled when Abby had called to beg her to come back to the ranch.

She'd still like her own place someday, a place to share with a special man. Immediately a vision of Derek's house filled her mind. It was designed to fill the imagination, encourage creative decorating, not as a cold, uncaring house, but rather as a warm, inviting home.

"All set." Janice interrupted her thoughts as she walked out of the bedroom clad in a pair of jeans and a bulky multicolored sweater.

"Great, I'm starving."

The two left the apartment and got into Belinda's car. "I've got something to tell you," Janice said as Belinda headed for the popular diner halfway between the city of Cheyenne and the Connor ranch. She wrapped her arms around herself and smiled. "I've been seeing somebody, and I think this time it's the real thing."

"Who?" Belinda knew her friend had a penchant for getting involved with losers, and hoped her new flame wasn't married, mean, or unemployed.

"It's somebody you know," Janice said coyly.

"Well, that narrows it down, since I know most everyone in Cheyenne," Belinda said dryly.

Janice giggled. "Okay, I'll narrow it down more. It's somebody who works at your ranch."

Belinda frowned, running through all the workers

in her mind. "Please, don't tell me you've gotten yourself involved with Billy Sims."

"No way," Janice scoffed. "Billy Sims has more problems than I can deal with." She hesitated a moment, a wide grin on her lips. "It's Roger."

"Roger?" Belinda turned into the diner parking lot, wondering if Janice knew about Roger's background, the fact that his father was a senator.

"Roger Eaton. I know it's crazy. I always wanted to fall for a man who owned a ranch, not one who worked on one, but somehow this time my heart is doing the talking instead of my head."

"Janice, I'm so happy for you," Belinda said. Apparently Roger hadn't told Janice his real identity. Somehow this struck a romantic chord in Belinda. Roger probably wanted to see if Janice could fall in love with him as a ranch hand before telling her he was the son of a prominent senator.

"It's early in the game still," Janice said once the two were seated at a booth inside the busy diner. "We've only been seeing each other for the past week." Her eyes sparkled with excitement. "But already I feel for him things I've never felt for anyone else before."

Belinda reached across the table and touched her friend's hand. "Truly, I'm happy for you. Roger seems like a really nice man."

Janice nodded. "You know when he'll be back in town? He called to tell me he had to leave on a family emergency, something about his father being ill."

"That's right, but we don't know for sure when he'll be back."

Their conversation was interrupted by the waitress

who took their orders. "So, when are we going to find a good man for you?" Janice asked once the waitress had poured them each coffee then departed.

Belinda laughed. "Just because you think you've found true love, don't think you should be playing matchmaker for me."

"Well, well, if it isn't two of Cheyenne's prettiest ladies," a deep voice boomed.

Belinda smiled at Teddy King as he sank next to Janice on the bench seat. "Hi, Bear. You're getting a late start this morning, aren't you?"

"Hell, no. I've been out at Derek's place since the break of dawn. I decided I deserved a coffee break." He grinned at the two women. "So what are you both doing up and out so early?"

"Belinda woke me up and dragged me here for breakfast," Janice explained. "You know these ranch women, up before the chickens."

Belinda laughed. "Actually, I got up early to see my family off. They all left for California this morning and once they were gone I decided to rouse Janice out of bed."

"How are things coming on Derek's house?" Janice asked.

"Terrific. We're just doing the finish-up work. Derek is happy, my workers are happy, and my bank book is happy."

"You all must have worked long hours to get the house finished so quickly," Belinda said.

Bear nodded. "Killer hours for the most part."

"You going to take a vacation when it's all finished?" Janice asked.

Bear laughed. "No way. I've got more work lined

up than I know what to do with. Business is booming.'' He looked at his watch and frowned. ''As a matter of fact, I've got to get.''

''No rest for the wicked,'' Janice exclaimed.

Bear laughed again and stood. ''You should know, sweetheart,'' he said with a wink, then turned and left.

''He's such a sweetie,'' Belinda said when he'd gone.

''Yeah, he and I dated for a little while a couple of years ago, but there was no chemistry…no spark. You know what I mean,'' Janice said.

The conversation halted as the waitress brought their breakfast orders. Belinda knew exactly what Janice meant about a missing spark. She'd had a few casual dates in the past six months, but no man she'd been out with had managed to stir the kind of spark Derek had in her.

With Derek it had been more than a sexual thing, although certainly their passion for each other had been intense. Still, what she'd felt for Derek had transcended physical attraction. She'd given him not only her heart, but her soul—and no other man had touched her deep within since him.

''Bear sure is doing great with his construction business.'' Janice picked up the conversation where they had left off.

''Yes, he seems to be quite successful.''

''The best thing that ever happened to him was his dad selling the hardware store to that big chain. He told me once that it was that sale that got the money for him to set up his construction business.''

Belinda frowned thoughtfully, an old memory niggling at the back of her mind. "Didn't Derek's father and Bear's father work together a long time ago?"

Janice nodded. "They were co-owners of the hardware store. From what I remember hearing at the time, Derek's father sold his shares to Bear's father right after the fire. Probably needed the money to help his family relocate."

"And then the chain bought out Bear's dad about a month later, right?" Belinda asked, reaching into the far corners of her mind.

"Yeah, I think that's right. Why?" Janice looked at her quizzically.

Belinda shrugged. "I'm just checking my memory."

"You'd better check out your omelet before it gets cold," Janice observed. "There's nothing worse than cold eggs for breakfast."

Janice did everything with gusto. As she attacked her breakfast with single-mindedness, the conversation waned. Grateful for the relative silence, Belinda picked at her omelet as her mind whirled with new suppositions.

She'd forgotten about the hardware store sale and how Derek's father had refused to sell...until after the night of the fire. Gossip at the time had it that the major chain had made a generous offer to buy them out, but Derek's father wasn't interested. Derek's father and Bear's father had been at odds over the potential sale.

Surely the thoughts zooming around in her head were crazy ones. Surely the fire that had destroyed Derek's home hadn't been set to threaten his father into the sale of the hardware store.

Still, the bullets the night before could have been just as easily meant for Derek as for her. Perhaps somebody was afraid he'd delve too deeply into the arson, discover the culprit and seek legal revenge.

If Bear's father was responsible, how much did Bear know? Everyone had always known how close Bear and his father were.

As Belinda dug deeper into her memory, she contemplated the friendship between Derek and Bear. They had been best friends forever, but their relationship had been tinged with more than a touch of competitiveness.

Was it possible Bear wasn't the best friend Derek thought him to be? Rather, was it possible Bear and his father had been responsible for the fire years before and now intended to cover their tracks by killing Derek?

Chapter Seven

Belinda rolled over and grabbed the phone from her bedside stand to stop the jangling ring that had awakened her. Sitting up, she breathed a sleepy hello into the receiver.

"Belinda? Did I wake you?" Abby's voice drifted over the line.

"No...I mean yes, but that's okay. What time is it?" Belinda asked, disoriented from her heavy sleep.

"Just a few minutes after nine. I had no idea you'd already be in bed."

"I came to bed about half an hour ago and must have fallen asleep immediately." Belinda turned on the lamp next to her bed in an effort to dispel the last of her sleepiness. "How are things going there?"

A pregnant pause followed the question and Belinda's heart sank. It had been three days since her family had left for California and she'd hoped that when she heard back from them they would have good news. The heavy silence spoke volumes.

"Not good, huh," Belinda said softly.

"No, not good." Abby's voice was thick with barely held emotion. "We've talked to several potential investors, but nobody seems interested in investing in us.'' There was another long pause. ''Oh, Belinda, I've never felt so hopeless.''

Belinda's heart ached with her sister's pain and with her own. ''When are you coming back?''

Abby cleared her throat, as if swallowing against a torrent of tears. ''We've got a few more appointments lined up in the next couple of days, although they're all long shots. We'll probably head back this weekend.''

''Abby, don't give up. Maybe one of the long shots will surprise us.'' Belinda wished she had more words of comfort to give her sister, but everything she thought of saying rang hollow in her own brain.

''Maybe. So, how's everything there? Any problems?''

''No, you have nothing to worry about here,'' Belinda assured her. ''Roger got back yesterday. Apparently his father is stabilized, but not in very good shape.''

''And you haven't run across those missing adoption papers anywhere?''

''No, although I'm still looking.''

Abby sighed. ''I know finding those papers is important to Roger, but at the moment I can't focus too much energy on that. My main concern is keeping our home.'' She sighed once more. ''I'll let you go back to sleep. I just wanted to check in with you and let you know how things stand so far.''

''I'm glad you called, I've been anxious to hear from you.'' Belinda squeezed the receiver tightly, wishing her sister was close enough for her to offer a reassuring hug. ''Abby, we're not going to lose our home. One way or another, everything will be fine. I promise.''

When Belinda hung up, it wasn't Abby's voice that reverberated in her head, rather it was Derek's and his crazy proposal.

She got out of bed and padded down the hallway to the kitchen, too wired to go back to sleep. Once there, she made herself a sandwich and sat at the table.

The ability to save the ranch rested in her hands. All she had to do was agree to Derek's cold, unemotional marriage proposal.

For the first time since he'd uttered the outrageous idea, Belinda found herself considering all it would entail. He'd said the marriage would be valid until the adoptions of his niece and nephew were finalized. How long could that take? Six months? A year at the most?

She was young, sacrificing a year of her life to save the ranch seemed a relatively small price to pay. What worried her was what else she might sacrifice in living with Derek, pretending to be his bride and mothering the two children he seemed to love.

Guilt battled with despair and she pushed her sandwich aside, no longer hungry. Yes, she could solve their financial problem—but at what cost to herself? Still, the overwhelming sadness in Abby's voice replayed mournfully in her mind and plucked at Belinda's heart.

If she didn't marry Derek and if Abby didn't find the investors needed, they would not only lose the ranch, but in all probability they would each go their own way. Luke and Abby and little Cody would build a life together, as would Colette and Hank and their baby girl.

"And what will I do?" Her words hung in the silence of the empty house. What would she do? Where would she go? She understood Bulldog's fear, for she felt the same emotion churning inside her as she contemplated life without the ranch.

The weight of the knowledge that she could solve everything merely by agreeing to Derek's proposition felt like a lead ball in the pit of her stomach.

She rubbed a hand over her eyes, too tired to make a rational decision tonight. Tomorrow she'd make a final decision. Tomorrow she'd decide if she could sacrifice her imminent future in exchange for assuring the continuing future of their home.

She left the kitchen and went to her bedroom. She sank into the softness of her mattress. She hadn't seen much of Derek for the past three days, although a dozen furniture and appliance store trucks had passed her house on the way to his.

She rolled over onto her back and stared up, where the moonlight filtering through the curtains cast dancing shadows on the ceiling. Within moments, she slept.

Almost immediately she began to dream, the familiar dream of Derek...and fire. They were stretched out side by side in a field of wildflowers and sweet-smelling grass. His lips captured hers in deep, soulful kisses, and his hands stroked rivers of desire to flood through her veins. The flames that surrounded them inched closer, close enough that she couldn't tell whether it was the proximity of the fire that burned her or Derek's passionate caresses.

As the fire edged closer, their lovemaking grew more intense and Belinda realized if they didn't stop, if they didn't run, the fire would consume them both.

She struggled against him, but he held her tight, so tight she could feel the frantic pounding of his heart. Sweat bathed both their bodies and her skin felt flushed, taut from the heat surrounding them.

Outside the ring of fire, her sisters stood, urging her to stay with Derek, save the ranch for their children and their childrens' children.

She awakened with a gasp, her legs tangled in the bed covers, her heartbeat pulsing at her temples. Remaining unmoving, she drew in several deep breaths in an attempt to slow her heart, slough off the remnants of the nightmare.

Her breath caught in her throat as an alien noise broke the silence of the night. She froze, willing herself to stop breathing and listen. A thud, followed by the soft tinkle of breaking glass. A window breaking? Was somebody in the house?

Each muscle in her body tensed. Making no sound, she swung her legs over the side of the bed and stood, searching in the moonlight for something that could be used as a weapon.

For the first time in her life she was sorry her father hadn't been a proponent of handguns. The only guns in the house were two shotguns in her parents' old bedroom.

Scanning the top of her dresser, she frowned at the perfume bottles and makeup, no bottle or container big enough to be hefted over her head and used in defense. She grabbed a can of hair spray, oddly comforted by the mere act of holding something—anything—in her hand.

She briefly considered hiding in the closet, but a vision of being trapped in the small confines by an attacker made her dismiss the idea.

Holding her breath once again, she peeked out her bedroom door and down the long, shadowy hallway. Nothing. Nobody. Maybe a tree branch had knocked against a window. Perhaps one of the glass knick-knacks in one of the bedrooms had fallen and crashed to the floor. Maybe nobody at all was in the house.

She stepped out into the hallway, her finger on the nozzle of the can she held. Slowly, cautiously, she made her way down the dark corridor. Once again her heartbeat thrummed in her temples, the rapid, aching beat of fear.

Passing the first bedroom off the hallway, she looked inside. Nothing amiss. No shattered window, no broken knickknacks.

She moved on to the second bedroom. As she reached the doorway, cold night air caressed her face. She stepped into the room and immediately spied the broken window. Shards of glass littered the carpeting, shining like gems in the moonlight. At this particular window there was no tree, no branches that might have accidently crashed into the glass.

Somebody did this. Somebody is in the house. The words of alarm screamed in her head. A rustling sound behind her caused her to whirl around. A black-clothed figure, face hidden beneath a ski mask, stood in the doorway.

"Who are you? What do you want?" Belinda shouted.

The intruder raised a hand overhead, the moonlight glinting on a knife. Belinda froze, watching in horror as the assailant began to advance.

All rational thought left her mind as survival instincts kicked in. She crouched, making herself as small a target as possible, at the same time looking around for a weapon better than the hair spray can.

Cold air poured through the window at her back, but perspiration dotted her skin as she watched her attacker draw closer. "What do you want?" she repeated. "Just take what you want and go."

Still the dark-clad figure advanced. Reaching out to the nearby table, Belinda picked up what she could and threw it. A paperback book. A box of tissues. A candle in a thick jar. The assailant easily dodged each item, continuing toward Belinda with frightening single-mindedness.

Despite Belinda's desire to scream—to run—she knew if she panicked, she would die. Instead she held her ground, waiting until the figure was close enough to strike. As the knife arced toward her, Belinda pressed the nozzle of the can, directing the spray into the eye slits of the mask. A white-hot pain riveted through Belinda as the knife glanced off her shoulder. Still, she directed the spray, sobbing in relief as the knife clattered to the floor and her assailant also fell to the floor, rubbing his eyes.

Belinda dropped the can and without hesitation dove through the window. She hit the ground on hands and knees, but instantly got up and took off running.

She didn't look behind her, didn't consider stopping as she ran past the bunkhouse. There was only one place she'd feel safe, only one person she truly trusted, and she headed there, running like the wind.

Her white nightgown billowed as she ran and she prayed it didn't act as a beacon to whoever might be chasing her. Her bare feet flew over the land, unmindful of rocks and brambles.

She didn't stop running until she reached Derek's front door. Pounding with her fists, she screamed his name. Hoping, praying he was home. Hoping, praying he would keep her safe.

DEREK AWAKENED to the banging on his door, immediately eyeing the luminous hands on the clock next to his bed. Two o'clock. He'd been in bed less than an hour.

"Derek!"

Belinda's voice reached him. Frantic with fear, it instantly propelled him out of bed. He yanked on a pair of jeans and raced down the stairway.

He disarmed the new security system and pulled open the front door. She collapsed into his arms. "Belinda. Dear God, what happened?"

He held her at arm's length, his gaze riveted on the red splash of blood that oozed from her shoulder and stained the white of her nightgown. He could instantly tell the wound was wicked, but not life-threatening.

She looked down at herself, then back at him, her eyes blackened with fear and near shock. As sobs racked her body he led her to the kitchen and sat her at the rich, oak table, then rummaged beneath the sink and withdrew a first-aid kit.

His hands trembled as he took out a bottle of hydrogen peroxide and cotton balls. Questions assailed him, but at the moment she was obviously in no condition to answer them.

"Shh, you're all right now," he murmured soothingly as he slipped her shoulder strap down to expose the slash that caused the blood flow.

"I—I didn't know where else to go...what else to do..." Any further words were drowned out as she once again sobbed.

"Don't try to talk now. Let me clean you up, then we'll talk," Derek said. Gently, he wiped the cotton ball over the wound. He breathed a silent sigh of thanks as he saw that the injury was already beginning to stop bleeding.

He worked silently, efficiently, trying to ignore the sweet floral scent that emanated from her. What had happened? Had she somehow cut herself, then panicked when the blood flowed? By the time he had the wound completely cleaned, she'd calmed down enough to talk.

He placed a bandage on the cut, then pulled a chair in front of her and sat. "Now, tell me what happened. How did you hurt yourself?"

"I didn't hurt myself." In her eyes, her lovely blue eyes, he saw fear. Her words caused adrenaline to pump through him.

"What happened?"

"I—I was asleep, having a nightmare, and I woke up. I was trying to fall back to sleep when I heard a thud, then breaking glass." She shivered, her eyes once again welling with tears.

He took her trembling hands in his. She clutched his tightly and drew in a deep breath, then continued. "I left my bedroom to see what had happened. The window in Abby and Luke's room had been broken. Before I could figure out exactly how it had happened, somebody attacked me...tried to stab me.''

Derek swallowed a curse bred from impotent helplessness. He'd been watching her house every night since her family had left town, not liking the idea of her being all alone. It had been sheer exhaustion that had driven him back home in the wee hours of each morning. This night had been no different, although the exhaustion had caught up with him earlier, driving him home from her place around midnight.

She winced and Derek realized he was squeezing her hands too tightly. ''Sorry...'' He released the pressure, but didn't let go of her hands. ''Go on,'' he urged. ''Tell me everything that happened.''

''Whoever it was, had on a ski mask. I had a can of hair spray and when he got close enough to try to stab me, I sprayed him in the eyes, then dove out the window and ran here.''

Derek stood and went to the phone and quickly punched in a series of numbers.

''Who are you calling?'' Belinda asked, her voice still trembling from the shock and terror she'd experienced.

''Junior. You've got to make a report of all this.''

''I don't want to go back there...at least not for tonight.'' Her eyes were huge, radiating a vulnerability that made Derek more determined than ever that nothing and nobody would ever harm her again.

''You can stay here for the rest of the night,'' he replied, then spoke into the phone, explaining the situation to the groggy, half-asleep sheriff.

''I'm to meet him at your house in fifteen

minutes,'' Derek said to her as he hung up the phone. ''I'm sure he'll want to question you, but he can do it here.''

She nodded, then shivered and wrapped her arms around her shoulders. Her fingers plucked nervously at the bandage over the wound. ''I—I just wish I could tell Junior who it was, but it was too dark and I was too scared to pay attention to any details.''

''You did the right thing in getting out of there. How about a cup of coffee before I leave to meet Junior?'' She nodded and Derek busied himself preparing the coffeemaker.

What he wanted to do was take her in his arms, hold her until her frightened shivering stopped and another kind of trembling began. He wanted to wrap his fingers in the golden spill of her hair, kiss her mouth until it was swollen. But he knew that was the want, the need, of the man he'd once been and had nothing to do with the man he was now.

He poured them each a cup of coffee, then joined her at the table. ''If you want to get out of that nightgown, there are T-shirts and sweatpants upstairs in the master closet. You can help yourself.''

''You think you'll be gone long?''

He heard the fear once again in her voice, knew she dreaded staying in his big house all alone for any length of time. ''Belinda, I've got a security system that covers every door and every window. If anyone tries to get in, an alarm will sound that's so loud, Junior and I will hear it at your place. I'll arm it as I leave.'' He reached out and touched her hand, his fingers stroking her knuckles. ''I promise you'll be fine.''

Her fingers closed around his. "Thank you, Derek." Her cheeks pinkened slightly. "I knew I'd be safe here with you." She released her hold on his hand and instead wrapped her fingers around her coffee mug.

"I'd better head out," Derek said as he rose from the table. "I want to be there when Junior arrives."

She walked with him to the door, where he punched in a code on the security control panel. "You'll be fine until we get back," he said, then left.

He opted for walking rather than driving to Belinda's. The chill night air caused his leg to ache more intensely than usual, but he ignored the pain, instead focusing his thoughts on Belinda and who might have attacked her.

He wondered, Who knew her family was out of town? Who had known she would be at the house all alone? Dammit, who was responsible for this latest attack and why...why did somebody want to hurt her?

There was no way to mistake the attack tonight as an accident, no way to assume it was meant for anyone other than Belinda. Who was it and why had Derek received the notes warning him of the danger to her? It seemed as if not only did somebody want to kill Belinda, but that somebody wanted to make sure Derek was a witness to her death. His blood ran cold at the very thought.

As the Connor ranch came into view, he was unsurprised to see that Junior hadn't yet arrived. He stopped some distance from the house, scanning the area intently, looking for anything amiss.

The cloudless sky allowed the light from the quarter moon to dust the house in silvery hues. All appeared quiet...normal.

He eyed the surrounding wooded area, the dark, silent bunkhouse and the rest of the outbuildings. Nothing seemed out of place, nothing out of the ordinary caught his eye. Still, he approached cautiously, knowing the shadows of night could hide things from view.

Instead of investigating on his own, he went directly to the porch and sat to await Junior's arrival. Derek was no cop and didn't want to disturb any evidence Junior's seasoned eyes might discover.

Within minutes Junior's patrol car pulled up the drive. Derek was grateful the old man didn't have the lights flashing and siren blaring. No sense in stirring all the workers, who could only add to the confusion.

"I hope this middle-of-the-night stuff with you and Belinda isn't going to become a habit," Junior grumbled as he unfolded his tall length from the car.

"I'm not exactly pleased to be here, either," Derek observed dryly.

"Where's Belinda?"

"At my place. She was shaken up, scared, and didn't want to come back here. I told her you can talk to her at my house after we take a look around here."

Junior nodded and placed a hand on the butt of his holstered gun. "Let's see what we find."

The front door was locked and appeared undisturbed. The two men walked around to the side of the house and instantly spied the broken window. "There." Derek pointed to a thick piece of wood just beneath the window. "Looks like that was used to smash in the window."

Junior pulled on gloves, then picked up the piece

of wood. "I'm going to put this into the trunk of my car. I'll be right back." He handed Derek his flashlight, then disappeared around the corner of the house.

While Derek waited for his return, he directed the beam of light along the bottom of the window. The jagged edge of remaining glass had snagged several dark threads. Derek remembered Belinda saying the intruder had been dressed all in black. It was obvious this was the point of entry.

When Junior returned, Derek pointed out the black threads, which the sheriff collected in a small evidence bag. They looked around the outside of the house for anything else that might identify the assailant, but found nothing.

All the doors were locked and rather than breaking one down to get inside, Junior suggested Derek enter through the broken window, then unlock the front door to admit him.

Careful not to cut himself on the pieces of glass the window still retained, Derek lifted himself up and through the opening. Shards of glass crunched beneath his feet as he stepped into the bedroom. He didn't stop to look around, but went right to the front door to unlock it and let the sheriff in.

"The first thing we'll do is make sure nobody is still here," Junior said. "Although I'm sure whoever did this isn't still hanging around."

Together the two men went from room to room, turning on lights and checking any space where a person could hide. They found nobody. What they did find was a burlap bag in the middle of the living room floor. Inside the bag was a pair of silver candlesticks, a gold-plated mirror and several collector figurines.

"Looks like Belinda surprised a burglar," Junior observed. "Probably some lowlife who heard she'd be out here all by herself."

"Maybe." Derek couldn't keep the skepticism from his voice.

Junior eyed him curiously. "You don't think so?"

Derek raked a hand through his hair, then rubbed his thigh thoughtfully. "Why would a burglar choose to take this stuff and leave the television, the stereo and that stack of Cody's computer games?"

Junior shrugged. "Maybe he intended to get the other stuff but before he could, Belinda woke up."

"Maybe," Derek repeated, not convinced.

"What do you think? That somebody wanted us to think it was just a burglary, but the real motive was to attack Belinda?" Junior heaved a deep sigh. "Have you told her about those notes you received?"

"No."

"I think it's time you do, don't you?"

This time Derek sighed. He hadn't wanted to tell her, had thought that by keeping her in the dark he was somehow protecting her, making things easier on her.

In the recesses of his soul, he recognized that he'd been using her as bait. Whoever had sent him those notes knew about his relationship with Belinda years ago. That meant they knew about the fire that had destroyed his life, might be responsible for that fire.

He hadn't wanted Belinda to know because he hadn't wanted her changing her habits, becoming so cautious that the hunter stopped the hunt.

But the hunter had nearly succeeded tonight. Had Belinda not grabbed that can of hair spray, had not awakened at all, he knew she'd be dead. Yes, it was time to tell Belinda and hopefully by working together they could find the person who hated enough to kill.

Chapter Eight

Derek's house radiated a still silence after he left, but the glowing light on the security panel assuaged any lingering fears Belinda might have. She was safe here, as she'd known she would be.

She wandered around the living room, admiring the casual but attractive furniture Derek had chosen. By his choice of furnishings, he'd somehow managed to imbibe the large room with warmth, with a feeling of intimacy and home.

As she passed a mirror hanging on the wall, she paused in front of it, studying her reflection. Who might want to hurt her? Why would anyone attack her with a knife? She plucked at the bloodstained nightgown, suddenly wanting it off.

She turned from the mirror and went upstairs to the master bedroom, again amazed at the transformation of the room now complete with furniture. The color scheme was peach and blue, and Belinda wondered if when Derek had chosen these colors, he'd remembered that they were her favorites.

Walking into the huge closet, she instantly spied the T-shirts and sweatpants Derek had told her she could borrow. The shirts hung neatly on hangers, and several pairs of the cotton pants were folded on shelves.

Shrugging out of the nightgown, she pulled one of the T-shirts over her head, trying not to notice how the material smelled like Derek. The sweatpants were big, but comfortable. The nightgown she tossed in the wastebasket, knowing it was ruined.

In the bathroom she found a hairbrush and quickly braided her hair. The simple, mundane task soothed the last of her taut nerves.

Curious to see the rest of the rooms since the furniture had arrived, Belinda left the master suite and wandered down the hallway.

She entered the room Derek had told her would be Tasha's room. Her breath caught in her chest as she entered. It was a room from a fairy tale, done in pastel pinks and pale greens and oodles of ruffles. A child-size table and chairs sat in front of the window where the sun could stream in and light a tea party.

The house was ready, the rooms were prepared. The only thing lacking was a wife for Derek and children to bring life to the rooms. Again she thought of the proposition he'd made her.

Could she marry Derek, remain his wife until the adoption of the children was final and the ranch was stable, then walk away without her heart being touched? That's what frightened her more than anything—the prospect of having her heart broken once again.

She left Tasha's room and entered Toby's. Cowboys on bucking broncos rode the wallpaper banner around the edge of the ceiling. Wooden bunk beds covered with matching brown spreads added to the boyish appeal. A large, sturdy rocking horse sat in the corner, awaiting the touch of a miniature cowboy to bring him to life.

An unexpected pain ripped through Belinda as she touched the rocking horse's mane. She'd once dreamed of a horse much like this one. A rocking horse for her son. Her baby.

She sank onto the bottom bunk, arms wrapped tight around her stomach to still the hollow ache that resounded deep within. He would have been two now...toddling around, speaking a combination of baby gibberish and real words. She closed her eyes, tears oozing as she imagined chubby little arms around her neck, a slobbery kiss on her cheek.

If only she hadn't left for Kansas City when Derek had dumped her. If only she'd remained here, among her family, then maybe...just maybe, things would have been different.

Wiping away her tears, she stood and yelped as the top of her head connected with the bottom of the upper bunk. She rubbed her head, almost grateful for the physical pain that momentarily displaced her emotional pain.

She walked to the doorway, then hesitated, her gaze once again sweeping the room. She knew now. She knew it was possible for her to marry Derek and keep her heart safe from him. If she felt any wavering at all, any softening of her heart toward him, all she had to do was enter this bedroom and remember the little boy she'd lost.

She didn't know how long she stood there, engrossed in thought, when the sound of the front door opening pulled her back to the present.

"Belinda?" Derek's voice drifted up the stairs.

"Up here. I'll be right down," she answered. She turned off the light in the bedroom, then hurried down the stairs to where Derek and Junior awaited her. "Did you find out anything?" she asked.

Derek shook his head. "Nothing too helpful. We boarded up the broken window so the house is secure for now. Why don't we sit down with a cup of coffee? Junior has some questions to ask you."

Together the three of them sat at the kitchen table. While Derek poured the coffee, Junior pulled a notepad and pen from his pocket. "I want you to tell me everything that happened from the moment you woke up to the moment you ran here," he said.

As Belinda replayed those moments for the sheriff, her fear also replayed inside her. The whole thing had taken on the ambience of a nightmare. But even nightmares had the capability of producing intense fear. Her heart raced and her hands shook as she told Junior exactly what had happened.

Derek seemed to sense her internal fright. He sat next to her and took her trembling hands in his. Belinda didn't know whether to be irritated or grateful that his touch instantly soothed some of her fear.

"Could you tell about how tall the intruder was?" Junior asked when she'd finished telling him what had happened.

"It all happened so fast. I didn't pay attention to any details." She frowned, feeling stupid and inadequate. "Whoever it was, was taller than me."

"What about build? Thin, heavy...medium build?"

Again Belinda frowned. "Not heavy... I don't know, medium build, I guess." She forced a smile. "I'm not much help, am I?"

"It was dark. You were scared." Derek squeezed her hand. "Nobody expects anything from you."

She smiled at him gratefully. For the moment their past was just that—the past. She was grateful for his support now, when her family was far away and she needed somebody.

Junior stood and put his notepad and pen in his pocket. "Well, that about does it, at least for tonight. I'll send that stick we found to the Cheyenne lab, see if they can lift some fingerprints. Maybe then we'll know exactly who's responsible for all this mess."

While Derek walked the sheriff to the door, Belinda rinsed the coffee mugs and placed them in the dishwasher. When she turned around, Derek stood in the doorway, his expression inscrutable. "We need to talk," he said.

She nodded, not knowing what he wanted to talk about, but unsettled by the dark secrets that suddenly seemed to radiate from his eyes. She sank into her chair at the table and looked at him expectantly.

As he walked across the room to the table, his limp was more noticeable than usual. Again she wondered what had happened to cause the injury, but didn't feel comfortable in asking him.

Before he sat, he went to a drawer and pulled out several sheets of paper. "I'd hoped I wouldn't have to tell you about these. I didn't want to needlessly frighten you, but after tonight you have a right to know.''

"I don't understand. What are you talking about?'' She looked at him in confusion.

"Just look at these.'' He pushed the papers in front of her.

Belinda picked up the first one. "Belinda Connor Is In Danger.'' The words were written in bold, black marker. She looked up at Derek, then back at the letter, her heart starting to pound a rapid rhythm. "Wh-where did you get this?''

"That first one was mailed to me about a month before I moved back here. It was postmarked Cheyenne, but needless to say had no return address.''

"I—I don't understand. Who would send you something like this?''

"Read the rest of them,'' he said, his grim tone causing a roiling dread inside her.

She moved the first note aside and the next one glared at her. BELINDA CONNOR MUST DIE. Horror swept through her. ACCIDENTS HAPPEN—BELINDA IS GOING TO HAVE ONE. Then BELINDA IS AS GOOD AS DEAD. There was a total of five notes in all; five prophesies of her death.

"Is this all some kind of sick joke?'' She finally found her voice.

"I'd hoped it was a joke…one in very poor taste. But too many things have happened for us not to take these notes seriously.''

"These are what brought you back here? All the rest of it—the children, the judge, your need for a wife—was all lies?''

"No. That's all true.''

"Why didn't you tell me about these before now?" she asked, fighting the wave of anger building inside her. "I had a right to know about these. What kind of a game are you playing that you'd keep this from me?"

He flushed slightly beneath her glare. "At first I didn't tell you because I thought they might be just a terrible joke. Then I started wondering why, if somebody wanted to hurt you, they'd want to warn me before the fact." His eyes bore into hers with dark intensity. "Belinda, this isn't just about you, and it isn't just about me. It's about us. And if it's about us, then it has to be about something that happened three years ago when we were together."

"But what?" Belinda asked softly. She focused on the notes, the glaring words causing cold fingers to waltz up her spine.

"I'm beginning to think that somehow what's happening to you now and the fire three years ago are connected." His brows drew together in thought. "Initially, I didn't tie it all together, and I still don't know what connects them, but I think they are."

"But how?" She rubbed the center of her forehead, where a throb of confusion had awakened. "The fire that burned down your house had nothing to do with me."

"I don't know," he admitted.

For a moment a silence stretched between them. Belinda allowed her mind to drift backward in time, to that summer when she and Derek had discovered the joy of love, the pleasure of passion. It was crazy to believe that anything she and Derek might have done in youthful splendor would create the kind of maliciousness it took for somebody to set a fire, and three years later make attempts on her life.

She suddenly remembered the conversation she'd had earlier in the week with Janice. "Derek, what about Bear?"

He frowned. "What about him?"

"The other day Janice and I were talking, and she reminded me that Bear got the money for his business from his father after the sale of the hardware store."

"Yeah, so?"

"The way I remember the gossip at the time, Bear's father was pressuring your dad to sell him his half of the business, but your dad wasn't interested in selling."

"Dad enjoyed being a businessman, and prided himself on the little personal touches the store offered customers. He didn't want to sell, but the fire took his heart away." Derek's eyes darkened and in their shadows Belinda saw deep pain and the suspicion of a friend's betrayal.

She knew how close he and Bear had always been and she hated having to taint that friendship with the possibility of treachery, but at the moment nobody could be above suspicion.

He raked a hand through his hair, the gesture causing the short blond strands to stand on end. Still, the disarray did nothing to dispel his attractiveness. She fought the impulse to stroke down his hair, say something to alleviate the dark shadows of suspicion in his eyes.

"It doesn't make sense," he finally said. "If Bear or his father set the fire in order to get my father to sell, then what's happening now? How does that tie in with these notes? To the threats against you?''

''I don't know.'' She rubbed her forehead again, her headache blossoming with each moment that passed. ''I can't think anymore tonight.''

''You're right. It's late and we both could use a good night's sleep.'' Derek stood. ''Come on, I'll get you settled in the guest room, then we'll talk more in the morning.''

Belinda nodded, grateful for his mention of a guest room. When she'd told him she wanted to stay here for the night, she hadn't thought ahead to what the sleeping arrangements might be. At the moment she was exhausted enough that a pallet on the floor would be fine with her.

She followed him up the stairs to a small room she hadn't seen before. Furnished with a double bed and dresser drawers, the room was as impersonal as a motel room.

''I haven't done much in here yet,'' Derek said, as if reading her mind. ''But it should be adequate for a good night's sleep. The bathroom is just across the hall and if you need anything else, just knock on my door.''

''Thank you, Derek. I don't know what I would have done without your help tonight.''

He shrugged, as always his gaze dark and enigmatic. ''Good night, Belinda.'' He turned to walk away.

''Derek?'' Belinda's heart pounded unsteadily. He looked back at her. ''Your marriage proposition, is it still available?''

''Yeah, why?''

"I accept."

Before he could say another word, she closed the bedroom door and expelled a tremulous sigh. She'd done it. Heaven help her, the die was cast. She'd saved the ranch...she just hoped she could pay the price without sacrificing her soul.

DEREK STARED at the bedroom door a long moment after it was closed in his face. *I accept.* The words rang in his ears, creating myriad emotions to sweep through him. First and foremost was joy. With their marriage, the judge would have absolutely no reason not to release the children into his care.

He turned away from the guest room and stopped first at the bedroom he'd prepared for Tasha, then Toby's. He remained in the doorway of the little boy's room, for the first time hope filling his heart. Hope for the future.

He'd given up hoping for any happiness in his future when he'd spent those torturous days and nights in his hospital bed.

He'd remembered Belinda telling him how beautiful he was, stroking the length of his body in reverence. As he'd stared at his wounds day after day, watched his mother's face each time she looked at his leg, he'd put away his dreams of love and family.

But now, with Belinda's agreement to become his wife, part of those distant dreams would come true. He'd be the best father he could to those children and his house would be filled with love and laughter.

He moved away from Toby's room and went into the master suite. As he undressed for bed, he thought of how funny Fate could be. At one time he'd dreamed of being married to Belinda, having children and building a future based in love. The fire had destroyed those dreams, yet Fate had given him a twisted version of them. Unlike his youthful fantasies, their marriage would not be based on love or passion. There was no place in his heart for these emotions. Rather, their marriage was based on need, on convenience, and on the concept that once they each gained what they wanted, they'd go their separate ways.

With a frown, he turned off the light, then moved to the window. From this vantage point he could see the top of the crooked oak, although he couldn't see the Connor place.

If what he believed was true, that somehow he and Belinda were connected in the mind of somebody who wanted to harm Belinda, then what sort of repercussions would their marriage have?

This most recent attack on Belinda screamed of desperation. The incident with the driver who'd forced her off the road on the night of the Harvest Moon Dance could have been written off as an accident. A foolish drunk driving too fast. Even the shots that had been fired at them might possibly have been denoted as an accident. A careless hunter who hadn't realized where his bullets had traveled.

But there was no way to misconstrue what had happened tonight. Somebody had tried to kill Belinda and while some attempt had been made to make it look like a burglary turned homicide, Derek had no doubt that the sole motive for the break-in had been to kill Belinda.

He leaned his head against the windowpane and in

his mind he heard the ticking of an imaginary bomb. Whoever was after Belinda was cunning, and working off some master plan that made no sense, that had its basis in some kind of madness. Only madness could explain what was going on.

He sensed an approaching explosion, a heightened danger, felt the vibration of an advancing train. What scared the hell out of him was, he had the distinct feeling that he and Belinda were chained together on the railroad tracks.

Chapter Nine

Although Belinda was exhausted, it took her some time to unwind and fall asleep. When sleep finally came, it carried with it nightmare after nightmare. She dreamed of fire, of Derek, and of black-clad figures wielding wickedly sharp knives.

She awoke with the colors of dawn streaming in through the window and painting their warm hues on the walls. For a moment she was disoriented by the unfamiliar surroundings, then she remembered. She was at Derek's, in his guest room.

Sitting up, she pulled the rubber band from the end of her braid and ran her fingers through her hair to separate the strands. She'd forgotten to release it from the braid before she went to sleep.

Although she'd only had a couple hours of sleep, and that disturbed by bad dreams, she felt relatively rested. After a shower and a cup of coffee, she'd be ready to face the new day.

She got up and grabbed the jogging pants she'd taken off the night before from the top of the dresser. She pulled them on, below the T-shirt she'd slept in, then went across the hall to the guest bathroom.

Standing beneath the spray of the shower, she allowed her mind to roam free, trying to digest all that had happened the night before.

Why would somebody want to try to kill her? She shivered as she remembered those moments of facing the intruder. She turned the faucet to make the water warmer. Who would hate her enough to break in to her home and try to stab her? What had she done to warrant such hatred?

Who had sent those notes to Derek? How could the fire three years ago and what was happening to her now be connected? Each question brought no answers, rather merely evoked more questions.

After showering, she dressed once again in the T-shirt and sweatpants she'd borrowed from Derek, then headed for the stairs to go down to the kitchen.

As she walked down the staircase, she smelled the fragrant brew of freshly made coffee. Apparently Derek was awake, as well.

He sat at the kitchen table staring into the cup of coffee in front of him. For a moment she stood at the foot of the stairs, taking the opportunity to study him before he noticed her presence.

He'd probably had dozens of women in the years since leaving here. Women would find his clean-cut features and masculine build attractive.

Had he held another woman like he'd once held her? Whispered the same sweet promises, the same words of love? Had another woman believed those words and suffered the same kind of heartbreak that Belinda had?

She shoved aside these thoughts and walked toward

him. He looked up as she approached. "You didn't sleep long."

"Neither did you." She got herself a cup of coffee and joined him at the table. She tried not to notice how the early morning sun peeking in the window painted his bare chest in warm, golden hues.

"Too many questions going through my head," he answered. "I've tried and tried to make sense of everything, but I can't."

"Me, too," she admitted. She wrapped her fingers around the cup, seeking the warmth as her thoughts provoked a chill to sweep through her. "What frightens me is that I don't know how to protect myself against an unknown entity. How do you fight an anonymous opponent?"

"You trust no one. Not your friends, not your workers, not even your sisters."

Belinda looked at him aghast. "Surely you can't think Abby or Colette would have anything to do with this. If you think that, you're crazy."

"I'll tell you what's crazy. Somebody sending me those notes, that's crazy. Somebody trying to kill you, first by shooting at you, then with a knife, that's crazy." Sharp as gunfire, his words exploded out of him. "Until we know why all this is being done, we can't know who...and that means we trust nobody."

He leaned back in his chair and raked a hand through his hair. "No, Belinda, I really don't think your sisters have anything to do with any of this, but you have to stay on your toes, be suspicious of everyone."

Logically, she knew he was right, but she also knew with certainty there was no way her family was involved in any of this. She took a sip of her coffee, her mind once again whirling in a dozen different directions. "So, what do we do now?" she finally asked.

Derek stood and went to a drawer. "I think we start by making some lists," he explained as he withdrew a notebook and pen.

"Lists of what?"

"Of people." He sat once again at the table. "Potential suspects."

"I don't even know where to begin." She remembered their conversation from the night before. "Maybe you should start the list with Bear's name."

He frowned, a shadowed darkness blanketing the warm brown of his eyes. "He might be a suspect in the fire that burned us out, but what could he possibly have against you?"

"I don't know. But I don't know what anyone might have against me. Bear knew where you were living, he could have sent you those notes."

He looked at her for a long moment, then wrote Bear's name on the paper. "Okay. Let's talk about the workers on your ranch. Who worked for you three years ago that's still with you?"

"Derek, I don't see how any of those men would have anything to gain—"

"Indulge me," he interrupted her. "We have to start somewhere. At least if we write out some lists I'll feel like we're trying to do something."

"You're right," she agreed. "Okay..." She frowned thoughtfully. "This isn't going to be a very long list, you know how transient ranch help is." She pictured the workers in her mind, trying to remember who had been there three years before. "Bulldog, of course, and Billy Sims."

Derek wrote each name in the notebook. "Philip Weiss...and I think that's it." She flushed slightly. "We've been down to a skeleton crew for the last couple of months."

"What about Roger Eaton?"

"What about him? He's only been at the ranch for about six months."

"Isn't he the one who's professing to be a brother to one of you?"

Belinda nodded. "Junior checked him out and he's who he says he is. His father really is a senator who's ill. All Roger seems to want is to find out which of us is the senator's long-lost daughter. I can't imagine why he'd try to harm me and he certainly had no way of knowing about our relationship in order to send you those notes."

Derek nodded and stared at the three names she'd given him moments before. "Have you had run-ins with any of these men?"

She shook her head. "Bulldog has been upset, scared about us selling the ranch, but I can't imagine him trying to harm any of us."

"I think we can safely mark Bulldog off. He doesn't have the mental ability to pull off something like this." He drew a line through Bulldog's name.

"Philip Weiss is so old. He should have retired years ago, but he doesn't want to so Abby has kept him on."

"You don't have to be young to set a fire, or drive a car, or break into a house," Derek said gently. He got up and poured them each more coffee. "Billy

Sims...didn't we catch him one time spying on us?''
he asked as he sat.

"Oh, my gosh, I'd forgotten about that," Belinda
exclaimed. Now that he'd mentioned it, the memory
exploded in her mind. She and Derek had been in the
old shed just in back of his house. They'd met there
at dusk, sneaking away from their families to enjoy a
few moments alone.

As always between them, it had taken only a kiss
or two, only a single caress for passion to flare. And
in the middle of their passionate interlude, a noise had
alerted them to the fact that they were not alone in
the shed.

Apparently Billy had crawled behind a stack of old
crates to sleep off the effects of a bottle of cheap
whiskey. Belinda remembered at the time she wasn't
certain who was more surprised, she and Derek, or
Billy. He'd stumbled out of the shed, muttering and
cursing beneath his breath. Belinda and Derek had
dissolved into a fit of giggles that momentarily dis-
pelled their passion.

"It was about a month after that when the fire was
set," Derek said, breaking into Belinda's memories.

"But why would Billy want to set fire to your
ranch? We didn't tell anyone about him sleeping in
the shed. What would possibly make him do such a
thing?"

"As I recall, Billy spent more time drunk than sober. Who knows, maybe in some drunken state he
irrationally thought we would get him into trouble, or
cause him to lose his job—" Derek broke off, the
skeptical tone in his voice letting her know he didn't
believe his own reasoning.

"But Billy is sober now," Belinda said.

"Does he have any reason to be angry with you? Is it possible he's nursing some sort of grudge?"

"Nothing that I can think of...at least not with me personally."

"What do you mean, not with you personally?" Derek leaned forward, bringing with him a clean, recently showered scent mingling with the subtle aroma of his cologne.

Belinda frowned, irritated by the emotional, almost physical reaction she had to his familiar scent. She got up and began to pace, trying to ignore the sudden heat his familiar smell had stirred inside her. "A couple months ago Billy's drinking really got out of hand and Abby fired him," she said as she walked back and forth in front of the window.

"Then why is he still at your ranch?"

"He left for a couple of weeks, apparently tried to work elsewhere, but couldn't find anyone willing to hire him. He wrecked his truck, lost visitation to his children, then came back and begged Abby to rehire him. He promised to join a program to help him stay away from the booze. She agreed to give him another chance." She stopped pacing and looked at Derek once again. "If Billy Sims has a grudge, it would be against Abby, not me."

"But maybe in his twisted mind, the way to harm Abby is to hurt you. You're more vulnerable than Abby. You make an easier target," he observed.

"What does that mean?" Belinda asked, irritated at the notion that somehow Abby was stronger, better than her.

Derek grinned, as if he recognized her irritation and

understood it. He stood, walked over to her and gently touched her cheek with his index finger.

"Don't worry, I'm not casting aspersion on your character. I meant nothing personal. Abby and Colette are married, they have husbands and children around them, so are rarely alone. That makes them less vulnerable than you."

For a moment she was frozen, captured by the sensation of his finger slowly tracing back and forth along her jaw. He stood so close to her she could feel the heat radiating from his bare chest. Once again his sexy scent seemed to surround her. The combination made her head spin with memories and her body respond as if with a mind of its own.

His hand moved to the hollow of her throat, where she knew he would be able to feel the rapid pulse that beat there. "Of course, our marriage will make you less vulnerable." He leaned even closer, his breath warm in her ear. "This house is secure, and as long as there's danger, I'll never be far away from you. I'll keep you safe, Belinda. I swear I won't let anyone harm you."

Their gazes locked, and for a moment there was nothing else in Belinda's mind except the fire in his eyes. The fire of hunger...a hunger that flared in her, as well. Her breath caught, her pulse raced and more than anything she wanted him to kiss her.

It was her want—her need—that brought her back to reality. She stepped away from his caress, away from the heat of his bare chest. He dropped his hand, his smile faltering slightly. "I hope you don't intend to flinch away from my every touch once we're married."

"You said there would be no intimacy in the marriage," she countered, annoyed by the unsteadiness of her voice.

He nodded, his eyes shuttered from showing any and all emotion. "That's true, but I expect us to display a certain amount of mutual affection to maintain the facade for the public and for the children."

Belinda turned toward the window, where the colors of first dawn had transformed into the bright light of full morning. "I need to get home. The workers will be wondering what happened."

"I'll drive you." As he went to retrieve a shirt, Belinda remained in the kitchen staring out the window.

Although she would have preferred to walk home, she knew to do that would be incredibly foolish. And she had a feeling she'd already done the most incredibly foolish thing possible in agreeing to marrying Derek.

It took two days for them to prepare for the simple wedding. It wasn't flower-ordering or dress-shopping that stole the time away, but rather the hammering out of a prenuptial agreement.

Belinda wanted to make certain that Derek would follow through on his promise to invest in the ranch. She also wanted to ensure that when their temporary marriage ended, there would be no repercussions to her sisters or the financial welfare of the ranch.

Derek had his own agenda. He made sure the stipulation was that she remain in the marriage until the adoption of the children was finalized. Both of them agreed that the terms of the prenuptial agreement would remain a secret.

On the morning of the ceremony, Derek waited in the lobby of the city building where Justice Randall Turkington's office was housed. He stood at the windows, staring out at the street, watching for Belinda's car.

He'd dressed for the occasion in a charcoal suit and a dress shirt, the shirt collar tight enough to be uncomfortable. Looking at his watch, he frowned. It was nearly time for the ceremony, but it would be difficult to perform without a bride.

Maybe she'd changed her mind. Maybe she wouldn't show up. He knew he was taking advantage of her, preying on the financial weakness of their ranch to achieve his own goals. But somehow he felt as if they were merely puppets, fulfilling some sort of destiny that had been written in the stars.

The moment he'd gotten the first note threatening Belinda, the moment he'd uttered her name to the judge in charge of the custody case, he felt as if his fate had begun a spin out of his control.

He'd once dreamed of marrying Belinda, of building a life with her, but those dreams had evaporated in the searing heat of fire. Now the marriage to her was simply a vehicle to try to attain what dreams were left in the ashes of those flames.

And if she didn't marry him…somehow, some way, he'd do whatever it took to get custody of those kids. They had become his reason for living. They were the only people who made him forget he was less than a whole man.

He leaned toward the window as a familiar truck

pulled up and parked just outside the building. With an agility that belied his size, Bear got out of the truck and bounded up the stairs and through the door next to where Derek stood. He stopped in surprise as he saw Derek.

"Whoa...don't we look dapper," he exclaimed with a grin. He looked at the floral bouquet Derek held in his hand, then back at Derek, his eyes wide. "Don't tell me. She said yes."

Derek nodded and Bear clapped him on the back. "Why in the hell didn't you tell somebody? We'd have thrown you a bachelor party."

Derek smiled. "Somehow that didn't seem appropriate under the circumstances. And please, Bear...it's important to us that nobody know this is more of a business dealing than a real marriage."

Bear nodded and reached out to straighten Derek's tie. "Don't worry, buddy. Your business is nobody else's."

"So what are you doing here?" Derek asked.

"I've got a couple building permits to straighten out." Bear shook his head and frowned. "Bureaucracy, it makes me crazy."

"Yeah, but you seem to be doing pretty well." Derek eyed his friend curiously, the conversation he and Belinda'd had two nights before still fresh in his mind. "I'd say the fire at my place was the best thing that could have happened for you."

Bear's face paled slightly. "I guess you could say that, but I certainly don't like to think of my fortune being built on your family's misfortune."

"Life works out funny sometimes, doesn't it?" Derek tried to keep his voice light, but recognized the hollow ring.

Bear looked at Derek intently. "You're my best friend, Derek. If I could give you my leg, I would." His face colored slightly and he broke eye contact. "I've got to get upstairs and straighten out my permit mess. I'll see you later."

Derek watched as his friend disappeared into an awaiting elevator. Had Bear or his father had something to do with the fire? *If I could give you my leg, I would.* Had that been guilt talking? The guilt of a man responsible for Derek's injuries?

Bear knew his address in California. He could have been the one who sent the notes to Derek. But why would he want to hurt Belinda? It just didn't make sense. Nothing did.

Once again he turned his attention to the window, relieved to see Belinda's car pulling into a parking space. So she had come after all.

As she got out of the car, the sunlight danced on her pale hair, causing it to shimmer like spun gold. She hadn't braided it for the occasion, but rather wore it loose and flowing down her back. His fingers tingled, as if remembering the sensory pleasure of tangling in the soft, sweet-smelling strands.

Clad in a two-piece beige suit, she walked with purposeful strides through the front door. She stopped at the sight of him, and in her eyes he saw her doubts.

He could almost hear what whirled inside her head just by looking in her eyes. Certainly this arranged marriage had little to do with the youthful dreams they'd once shared of their wedding day. There would be no family, no friends, no white dress or reception. It would be just her and Derek and two paid witnesses watching their exchange of vows...vows based on need...vows based on lies.

"I wasn't sure you'd really go through with it," he said.

She smiled, the gesture not quite alleviating the shadows from her eyes. "I almost didn't. I had to fight to keep from turning around and driving back to the ranch."

"You won't regret this, Belinda. I swear, the time will go fast and we'll both get what we want." He held out the bouquet. "These are for you. Every bride should have flowers."

She took the bouquet of white roses and pale ribbon, her expression letting him know he'd touched her with the gesture. His heart suddenly felt too large for his chest, ached in a way he hadn't thought possible. For the first time, he wondered if he was making a mistake.

He'd believed he could do this...live each day with Belinda and not want her as he'd wanted her in the past. He'd thought he'd put those crazy, passionate emotions behind him, but apparently a residual remained to taunt him. He steeled himself against it. "Come on, we'd better go. They'll be waiting for us."

"Have you talked to your family?" he asked as they rode the elevator to the sixth floor.

She shook her head. "I haven't heard from them for a couple of days. I'm assuming they're on their way home."

"Do you think they'll believe that we fell madly back in love and impetuously decided to get married right away?"

"They'll believe it because they'll want to believe it. Both Abby and Colette are romantics at heart. They'll be disappointed that they missed the ceremony, but they'll be happy for me." Her gaze refused to meet his. "Later, when it's time, I'll simply pretend to fall out of love and we'll divorce like so many other couples do."

Although it was exactly what they'd agreed on, the words sounded cold when said aloud. The elevator doors opened and Derek put all his own doubts aside. It took them only a minute to find Justice Turkington's office. "Ready?" He took her hand in his, unsurprised to find hers cold as ice.

"Ready," she agreed, her voice faint. Together they stepped inside the office.

The ceremony was brief, and for Derek went by in a blur. The two witnesses, both elderly women, beamed their approval as Justice Randall Turkington solemnly performed the service.

"You may now kiss your bride," Justice Turkington said to Derek to indicate the end of the ritual.

He leaned down and captured Belinda's lips. He intended to make it a cool, perfunctory kiss, but the moment his mouth touched hers, he lost control. He didn't just kiss her, he took possession of her mouth, invading its sweetness with his tongue.

He was vaguely aware of the witnesses tittering but did nothing to end the kiss. Instead he wrapped his arms around her and pulled her more tightly against him. For this single moment, he wanted just to feel her close to him, taste her lips without rational thought interfering. For just this single moment in time, he wanted to feel like her husband in every sense of the word.

At first, she remained stiff and unyielding in his arms, but as the kiss continued, he felt her surrender as she leaned into him, her mouth eager and responsive.

He finally, reluctantly, broke the kiss. "Let's go home, Mrs. Walker." She nodded and together they left the office.

"I'll follow you to your place," he said as they walked to her car. "You can pack up whatever you need to move into my house."

"Derek, maybe it would be better if I just stay at home until Abby and Colette get back. You had the security system installed, so I should be safe."

"And how would that look to everyone? Belinda, we agreed that neither of us is eager for anyone to know the circumstances of our marriage. You don't want anyone to know you married me for money, and I'm not particularly eager for people to know I married you to gain custody."

Belinda flushed, and he knew it was because it all sounded so cold-blooded when boiled down to those simple facts. "You make me sound like a prostitute," she replied.

"We both know that's not true," he chided. "Besides, men don't usually marry prostitutes. They have sex with them, and I already promised you that sex won't be an issue in our relationship."

"You're right." She twisted the diamond ring he'd placed on her finger as if finding the feel of it uncomfortable. She leaned against her car door, studying him thoughtfully. "Odd how things work out, isn't it?"

He knew exactly what she was talking about, knew she was thinking the same things he had about the irony of Fate. "After the fire...why didn't you contact me?" The question had been on his mind for three long years.

She blinked in surprise. "How could I? I didn't know where you were. I called all the hospitals in Cheyenne, but nobody would tell me anything."

"Didn't my mother call you? Tell you where we were?"

She shook her head. "I didn't hear from your mother. I didn't hear from anyone until the day I got the letter from you."

Derek frowned, trying to dig through the distance of the past for the memories of those days and nights in the hospital. He remembered begging his mother to contact Belinda, to let her know where he was. He also remembered her noncommittal replies and knew in his heart what had happened.

She'd never called Belinda. His mother had probably believed she was protecting him, sheltering him from Belinda's revulsion. Dammit, how could his mother make that kind of decision for him? Still, it was difficult to maintain anger at her for trying to shield him from any more hurt.

The result was that Derek had believed Belinda hadn't cared enough to call him or see him. She'd only been toying with him, spending a summer with the boy next door. It had been that belief that had made him write the letter telling her she'd been nothing but a passing fancy to him.

"Why? What difference does it make now, after all this time?" she asked curiously.

Derek shrugged. "None. None whatsoever." He opened her car door to let her get in. "I'll be right behind you," he said.

Minutes later as he followed her car down the highway that led out of the city of Cheyenne and toward the rural area where they lived, Derek found himself replaying the conversation again in his mind.

So the reason Belinda hadn't contacted him after the fire was that she hadn't known where he was. It hadn't been because she didn't care.

Still, he'd answered her question truthfully. It no longer mattered. At that time, in the early days of his hospitalization when he'd been desperate to hear from her, see her face, he hadn't realized the extent of his injuries.

Derek faced the result of the fire daily, when he dressed or bathed. And even after all the time he'd had to adjust to the appearance of the scars, there were still days when looking at them made him ill.

Nothing could change the past, and he could never allow himself to love Belinda again. If he did...if he loved her enough to trust her, to reveal the extent of his injuries to her, he was afraid he'd see one of two things in her eyes: abhorrence or pity. If that happened, he'd grow to hate her.

No, he'd have to be content in living with the memories of loving Belinda and perhaps in indulging himself in fantasies of what might have been. He'd help save her home, hopefully they'd discover who burned him out and who was after her. He'd gain custody of his brother's children, then he'd let her go.

It was the right thing to do. The sane thing to do. What he didn't understand was why the thought of it caused an ache to pierce through his heart.

Chapter Ten

"I still can't believe this!" Abby hugged Belinda for the third time in as many minutes. As Abby released her, Belinda was immediately smothered in a hug from Colette.

Derek and Belinda had been at the house packing her things when Belinda's family had returned home from their long trip. Any exhaustion they might have felt from their extended time in the car seemed to disappear the moment Belinda told them about the marriage.

As her sisters squealed and hugged her, her brothers-in-law clapped Derek on the back and welcomed him into the family.

"We've got to plan a party to celebrate," Abby said. "We'll have a get-together here next Saturday night and invite all our friends."

"Oh, please, don't do that. It's too much trouble," Belinda protested. The last thing she wanted was a party to celebrate a sham of a marriage.

"It won't be trouble, it will be fun," Abby replied. "And I won't take no for an answer."

"Why didn't you wait to have the ceremony when

we got home?'' Colette asked. "I can't believe you guys didn't wait so we could all be at the wedding."

Derek placed an arm around Belinda's shoulder and pulled her close. "I'm afraid that's my fault. We just got a crazy impulse and I talked Belinda into surprising you." He gazed at Belinda, his eyes filled with warmth. "I wasn't going to wait another minute to make her mine."

Belinda's breath caught in her throat. Although she knew he was merely pretending, she was shocked to realize that for just a moment, she wanted the emotion emanating from his eyes to be real.

"Aunt Belinda, I got a shell on the beach and it whispers to me," Cody exclaimed.

Belinda stepped away from Derek's arm, grateful for Cody's interruption. She picked up the six-year-old, who wrapped his legs around her like a monkey. "A whispering seashell, that sounds pretty awesome."

"It is. I wanted to bring home a crab, but Mom said no way." He wiggled out of Belinda's arms and scrambled back to the car, where he reached in and withdrew the prized conch shell. "I want to show this to Bulldog."

"I think I saw him heading for the barn right before you all pulled up," Derek said.

Cody looked at his mother, who nodded her approval, then he tore off toward the barn, yelling Bulldog's name with every step.

"At least the trip was a definite success for one member of the family," Luke said as he took two suitcases out of the car trunk. He looked tired, disheartened, and Belinda knew how difficult it had been for both her brothers-in-law to want to help with the financial burden of the ranch but neither knew what else to do.

"Here, let me help you with one of those," Derek said as he took one of the suitcases from Luke.

"Yes, let's get these things inside, then I want to hear all the details of your whirlwind courtship," Abby exclaimed.

Hank carried Brook while Derek and Luke grabbed the suitcases. Within minutes they were all in the kitchen, everyone talking at once as they tried to catch each other up on the trip, the meetings they'd had, and the wedding that morning.

Belinda told them about the break-in, although she gave them the official version of a burglary interrupted. She also explained about the new security system Derek had had installed.

Abby asked if she'd found the missing adoption papers while they had been gone. Belinda shook her head. "But we've got more news," she said. "Derek wants to invest in the ranch."

They all turned and looked at Derek, who nodded and smiled. "It's true. I've got some money put away and have been looking for a good investment. I can't think of anything better than investing in my new family."

Abby's eyes welled up with tears. "Oh, Derek, I don't know what to say. It's like an answer to a prayer. I swear you won't be sorry. All we need is some capital to work with, buy grain for the fields that have lain fallow for so long. More cattle—we aren't utilizing half the pasture we've got because right now our herd is so small. You won't regret it, Derek...I swear."

"Abby." Luke took his wife's hand and smiled gently. "Just say thank you for now."

She laughed and cried at the same time, and as Belinda saw her sister's joy, she knew she'd done the right thing in agreeing to Derek's proposal.

"I'll have my lawyer draw up some papers and get them to you along with a check in the next couple of days," Derek said. "And now, I'm going to finish loading my bride's things so she can get settled at my place."

"I'll help you," Hank said as he handed Brook to Colette. "She's wet."

Colette laughed. "Of course. You always give her back to me when she's wet." She stood with the baby in her arms. "I'm going to go change a diaper, I'll be right back."

Luke joined Derek and Hank as they left, leaving Abby and Belinda alone in the kitchen. "Belinda." Abby reached across the table and took Belinda's hand in hers. "Tell me you didn't do anything foolish. Tell me you married Derek because you're desperately in love with him."

Belinda knew if Abby knew the truth, she'd refuse to take a cent from Derek. She summoned every ounce of acting skill she possessed. "Of course I'm in love with Derek. I think I've always loved him. Maybe some would say that our getting married this morning was rather foolish, but it made sense to us. We wanted to be together and we didn't want to wait to have a traditional wedding."

"So Derek investing didn't have anything to do

with your decision?'' Abby's blue eyes stared into Belinda's intently.

Belinda forced a light laugh. "I didn't even know he was going to offer until after the wedding ceremony. He said it was my wedding present."

The worry fell away from Abby's gaze and she breathed a deep sigh of relief. "I'm so happy for you. I know how crazy you were about Derek years ago. It seems so right, so romantic that you found each other again." She squeezed Belinda's hand.

"I've got another surprise. The family is going to expand by two very soon."

"Surely you aren't telling me you're already pregnant with twins?"

Belinda laughed. "No, nothing like that. Derek and I are going to adopt his brother's children. A five-year-old little girl and a four-year-old boy."

"That's wonderful. A ready-made family." Abby smiled. "Cody will be thrilled. Two new cousins and one of them a boy."

Colette came back in, Brook cooing happily in her arms. "So, sis, you and Derek have big plans for your wedding night tonight?" she asked. "Got a honeymoon planned?"

Belinda shook her head. "No honeymoon."

"But I've got a special night planned for my bride," Derek said from the doorway. "I've got everything loaded. Are you ready to go?"

Belinda wanted to say no, wanted to remain here in the safety of the kitchen. But she knew she couldn't do that. Legally, she was now Derek's wife. Intellectually, she knew it was important to keep up the facade. Emotionally, irrationally, she was suddenly scared as hell.

Swallowing hard against her fear, she kissed her sisters, then walked with Derek outside. Her car was loaded with clothes, toiletries, favorite books and shoes, everything she thought she'd need to begin her new life as Derek's wife for a year.

She followed Derek's car the short distance to his house and together they unloaded the items from her car and put them on the sofa in the living room.

"While you get your things put away and settle in, I've got to go back to town and fill out some paperwork for the judge in charge of the kids' case," he said. "I'll lock you in, so you should be fine, and I'll be back in an hour or so."

Belinda was grateful when he left. She needed some time to herself, time to get her thoughts and emotions under control. Derek playing the role of loving husband had unsettled her, made her realize just how difficult the next year might be.

As she carried her clothes up to the guest bedroom where she'd slept on the night of the break-in, she realized when her emotions had flown out of kilter. It had been when he'd asked her why she hadn't contacted him after the fire.

He'd implied that his mother was supposed to have called her, let her know where they were. But she'd never gotten a call.

She'd slept through the fire, unaware of the real-life drama playing out nearby. When she'd awakened the next morning, Derek's home was burned to the ground and she'd been frantic to find out where he was...if he was all right. Nobody seemed to know what had happened to him. It was only later, when she'd gotten his letter, that she realized he was with his family in California.

She went downstairs and grabbed another armload of things to take to the guest room, her mind still whirling. Had he written that horrible letter to her because he'd believed she'd known where he was and simply hadn't cared?

Back and forth, she went from the living room to the upstairs bedroom. Back and forth her mind flew from past to present, from memories to reality.

Try as she might, she could make no sense of the past. And in any case, as Derek had said, it no longer mattered. History was written, and there was no way to go back and change it. She'd loved him once, but that love was now tainted by a little white cross on a cemetery plot.

She was momentarily married to him, but she'd never allow herself to love him again. Her pain was too deep, her sorrow too wide for any love he had to offer to breach it.

She'd uphold her end of this crazy bargain. She'd play the role of loving wife to the public, and guard her heart against any intrusion in private.

Satisfied, she shoved all thoughts aside and focused on the simple task of arranging her clothes in the massive closet. She didn't realize how long she'd been working until she heard the distant sound of the front door creaking open.

"Derek? Is that you?" she called down the stairs.

"Yeah. You settling in all right? Finding everything you need?"

"I'm fine. Almost done. I'll be down in a few

minutes." She turned back to the closet and finished arranging.

"What are you doing in here?"

She whirled around at the sound of his voice. He stood in the doorway of the guest room. "What do you mean? This is where I stayed before. I just assumed..." Her voice trailed off as she noted his clenched jaw. "Surely you don't intend for me to share your bedroom?"

"Husbands and wives generally share the same room. We're adults, Belinda, and the bed in my room is a king-size one. We should be able to sleep together without too much discomfort. Besides, I don't want to give the kids a warped perception of marriage by sleeping in separate rooms."

"Yes, but I don't think..."

"You can stay in here for now, but when the children arrive, I expect you to move into the master bedroom." Without waiting for her reply, he turned and disappeared down the hallway.

"I WISH Abby and Colette hadn't pursued this party idea," Belinda said as she and Derek got into his car to drive to the Connor ranch.

"You know this is something they wanted to do," he observed.

"Yes, but it's so awkward. What if somebody brings us a wedding gift?" Belinda nervously toyed with the belt on her hunter green coat.

"You graciously thank them," Derek answered. He flipped the fan on the heater, sending warm air down to their feet. "Belinda, I'm sure over the next year we'll be faced with lots of social occasions.

Surely you can summon up the strength to behave like a loving newlywed when in public.''

"Don't worry, by the time this is all over you'll want to buy me my own Academy Award.''

Derek laughed, a pleasant rumble that filled the interior of the car with warmth as effectively as the heater.

Belinda leaned her head back and stared out into the night. Darkness fell earlier and earlier with winter's swift approach.

Winter had already arrived at the Walker house, at least as far as the temperature between husband and wife. They'd spent the past week in polite coolness, careful not to invade each other's private space. The only real time they spent together was each evening after supper when they sat at the kitchen table and went over and over their list of suspects.

Still, Belinda went to bed each night with his scent eddying in her head and her dreams had changed from frightening nightmares to tormenting memories from their past.

"Good grief, Abby and Colette must have invited half of all Cheyenne," Belinda said as they approached the ranch and she saw all the cars parked in the front yard.

Derek found an empty spot and pulled in. Together they got out of the car and walked toward the porch. Before they reached the front door, Derek took her hand and pulled her close against him. "I didn't tell you before we left, but you look beautiful tonight.'' Without warning, he kissed her. Deeply. Hungrily. His hands moved up her back, tangling in her hair as he took possession of her mouth.

Belinda was vaguely aware of the opening of the front door. "I thought I heard a car," Luke said, amusement evident in his tone. "It's the guests of honor," he announced.

"Okay you two lovebirds, break it up," Abby exclaimed.

Derek released her, a sheepish grin on his face. "Sorry, couldn't help myself."

As Luke and Abby ushered them inside, Belinda felt the flush that heated her cheeks, was intensely aware of a slight swelling to her lips that gave her a just-kissed appearance.

Belinda and Derek were immediately overwhelmed by congratulatory cheers and hugs from friends and neighbors. Glasses of champagne were passed around and toast after toast was made to the newlyweds.

There were three things Wyoming ranchers loved: their land, their livestock and a party. Once the official toasts had been made, somebody cranked up the stereo and the purpose of the party changed from congratulating Belinda and Derek to just having fun.

Derek and Belinda drifted from one cluster of people to the next until they had made the rounds of everyone. Belinda smiled until her teeth ached. Derek kept his arm around her shoulder, his hand caressing her hair as he joked and talked to their friends.

She wondered if he had any idea what his simple touch did to her, how it quickened her pulse, weakened her knees, made her blood course hotly through her veins. When she could stand it no longer, she excused herself and went to the kitchen for a soda.

Grateful to find nobody else in the kitchen, she took

a moment to lean against the counter and clear her head. Derek had thrown her thoughts and body into chaos with that kiss at the front door.

She could almost hate him for it. She could almost hate him for being able to pretend so easily. The fact that he could kiss her, touch her, gaze at her with his soulful brown eyes and not feel a thing for her made her both angry and sad.

What really worried her was that she recognized a small part of her that wanted his touch, wanted his kiss. There was a small part of her that still carried a remnant of love, although it was a part of herself she intended to suffocate, not nurture.

"Aren't you a sly one."

Belinda turned to see Janice as she walked into the kitchen. She gave Belinda a warm hug, then stepped back and shook her head. "Is your best friend always the last to know what's going on in your life?"

"I would have told you, but it all happened so fast," Belinda replied. She wanted to tell Janice the truth, that the entire marriage was a sham and that it was just a matter of time before it was over. But she knew if she did tell Janice, it wouldn't be long before all of Cheyenne knew. Janice was her best friend, but she was also a shameless gossip.

"I guess Derek knows how to be persuasive," Janice continued.

"Yes, very persuasive." Belinda felt a flush warm her cheeks. She hated playing this game, lying to her friends and family. But for them to know the truth—that she sold her soul to save the ranch—would be worse.

"Enough about me," she went on. "Derek and I

are old news now. Tell me what's going on with you. I saw you were with Roger.''

Janice nodded with a self-satisfied smile. ''We've been seeing each other every night since he got back from his trip. The man is crazy about me.''

Belinda laughed. ''So, will we be having another wedding soon?''

''Oh, I don't think so. It's too early for that. Roger and I are still getting to know each other. You know, sharing secret dreams and exploring possibilities.'' Janice smiled. ''It's amazing how much Roger and I have in common. I never, in my life, dreamed I'd meet a man like him.''

Belinda gave her a quick hug. ''I'm happy for you.''

''Ah, there you are,'' Abby said as she came into the kitchen. She smiled a greeting at Janice, then looked at her sister. ''You've got a tableful of gifts out there, and everyone is demanding you open them now. Colette is ready to record them as you and Derek unwrap them. Come on, everyone is waiting.''

Together the three women left the kitchen and minutes later Belinda and Derek began opening their wedding gifts. Silver platters and trays, a set of delicate wineglasses, bulky bath towels and pretty sheet sets. The traditional gifts were interspersed by gag gifts that kept the guests alternating between aahs of appreciation and hoots of laughter.

''Let them cut the cake,'' somebody shouted when the gifts had all been unwrapped.

''Yeah, cut the cake,'' another echoed.

Abby laughed and turned to Belinda and Derek. ''You hear them. Wait right here and I'll be back with the cake.'' She disappeared into the kitchen and returned moments later carrying a two-tier wedding cake complete with bride and groom figurines atop the white concoction.

"Oh, Abby, it's beautiful,'' Belinda exclaimed as her sister set the cake on the folding table that had held the gifts. "But you shouldn't have gone to so much trouble.''

"There's no such thing as too much trouble when it comes to my sisters,'' Abby replied.

Tears welled up in Belinda's eyes. Tears of love, tears of shame, tears of guilt. She hoped Abby and Colette never found out the real reason she'd married Derek.

"Let's get a few pictures before you cut the cake,'' Colette said as she handed Belinda a beribboned cake cutter. "Derek, move in next to her...you know what I want.''

Derek nodded and stepped close to Belinda. As she poised the knife across the top of the cake, he covered her hand with his. Cameras flashed and whirred as Abby and Colette captured the traditional wedding moments on film.

When the pictures were taken, Belinda cut a piece of cake and picked it up in her fingers to feed to Derek. The crowd coaxed her on, urging her to shove it in his face. She forced a laugh and shook her head. She just wanted the ritual over and done.

She held the cake to Derek's mouth. Delicately, he took a bite, but as she started to pull her hand away, he captured it with his and brought it back to his mouth. Slowly, sensually, he licked her fingers, then drew her index finger into his mouth to suck off the last of the sticky icing.

Belinda felt as if she were suffocating. The feel of his mouth around her finger caused a visceral pull deep within her. The people surrounding them seemed to fade away, and in that moment she knew she wanted Derek.

She breathed a shuddery sigh as he released her fingers, but tensed again as he picked up a piece of cake and directed it toward her lips. There was something primal, something almost savage yet symbiotic in the ritual of bride and groom feeding each other.

Derek's eyes blazed into hers as he guided the cake closer and closer to her mouth. She saw the sudden twinkle in their brown depths, the tiny smile that lit his features just before he smooshed the cake into her mouth, smearing it across one cheek.

She gasped and caught her breath as everyone laughed and clapped. Derek pulled her into his arms, his laughter ringing sweet in her ears. "I couldn't help myself," he said. To the crowd's delight, he licked her cheek and again desire winged through her, rich and vibrant.

Grateful when he released her, she grabbed a napkin and cleaned the last of the cake off her face, then busied herself helping Abby and Colette serve all the guests.

When everyone was served and there was a lull in the party, Belinda slipped back into the kitchen and out the back door, needing a few minutes alone to clear her thoughts.

Crisp and clean, the night air held the scent of approaching winter. Cold, snowy days, and frigid, lonely nights. The prospect of being cooped up in the house with Derek during the long winter months was daunting.

She wrapped her arms around herself and stepped off the back porch. The light from the near half moon spilled down to paint the land in a surreal silvery glow.

Warmth spread through her as she gazed at the familiar terrain. She remembered her father walking with his three daughters, his eyes glowing with pride as he surveyed his little kingdom. "My very own piece of heaven," he said, then smiled at each of them. "And I've got my own three little angels to prove it."

It didn't matter whether Belinda had been adopted or not, she'd never doubted his love for her and her sisters.

How he'd loved the land, and how he'd loved them. Belinda felt a soothing peace sweep over her as she realized her marriage to Derek had saved her father's dreams. The land would continue to be Connor land, passed from generation to generation.

She would survive this year of marriage to Derek. She'd do it for the father and mother who'd raised and loved her, for her sisters and their children.

All she had to do was figure out how to live with Derek, spend time with Derek and not want him. A deep heat swept over her as she thought of the kiss they'd shared, of the sensation of his tongue against her finger, against her cheek. He was wicked, positively wicked to do such a thing.

It has nothing to do with love, she told herself

firmly. Lust. That's all it was, pure and simple, un-complicated and base.

"Belinda." A voice called to her from the side of the porch.

"Who's there?" Belinda asked, the voice too faint for her to identify. "Derek, is that you?"

She stepped around the corner into the dark pool of shadows. She gasped as something dark and cool came down over her head. What was happening? What?

Plastic. It smothered her as she breathed in with panic. At the same time hands closed around her neck, squeezing painfully against her throat.

She pulled at the hands, at the same time kicking her feet in sheer terror. She couldn't breathe. Couldn't…breathe…

A choking, gurgling sound filled her head and she realized the noise came from her. She was listening to the sounds of her own death.

Tighter. Harder. The hands squeezed, cutting off all air and constricting her blood flow. She knew she should fight. But couldn't. Pinpoints of light exploded in front of her eyes as her knees buckled. A creeping numbness swept through her and she descended into the blackness of oblivion.

Chapter Eleven

Derek saw Belinda escape into the kitchen. As minutes passed and she didn't return to the party, he decided to go looking for her.

The kitchen was empty, but the back door stood ajar, letting him know she must have stepped outside for some fresh air. He could use a little himself. The house was uncomfortably warm with the press of people.

He walked out onto the back porch. "Belinda, are you out here?" he called. He waited a moment for his eyes to adjust to the relative darkness. The night was still, and he leaned against the railing, allowing the cool night air to blow gentle, refreshing fingers against his face.

It was obvious Belinda wasn't out here. Nobody was. She must be back in the living room and somehow he'd just missed seeing her. He turned to go back inside. Before he could reach the door, a faint noise made him pause.

He cocked his head, listening for the sound to be repeated. A minute passed. Two minutes. Then he heard it again. A soft moan.

His heart stopped. Blood rushed to his head as he jumped off the porch to investigate exactly what—or who—was making the noise.

He nearly tripped over her, so deep were the shadows that engulfed her. She lay unmoving, her head wrapped in something dark. "Belinda," her name choked out of him as he crouched beside her.

Plastic. Her head was covered in plastic. His fingers tore through what he instantly recognized as a garbage bag, freeing her face from its confines.

Her eyes snapped open and she flailed wildly, kicking her feet and swinging her arms to ward him off. Pitiful, terror-filled whimpers escaped her and he realized she wasn't seeing him, but was still fighting whoever had attacked her in the first place.

"Belinda. Belinda." He called her name sharply and watched with relief as her eyes finally focused on him.

She stopped her fighting and instead embraced him around the neck and buried her face in the front of his shirt. "Derek...he tried to kill me." The words came from her amid coughing and choking.

"Who? Who was it?"

She shook her head. "I don't know. I couldn't see."

He scooped her up into his arms, wanting to get her inside to the warmth, into the light where he could assure himself she was all right.

"What are you doing?" she asked as he started up the steps to the porch.

"Taking you inside."

"No!" She stiffened in protest. "No, please, let's just go home."

Near hysteria made her voice more high-pitched than usual and Derek realized she was on the verge of shock. "Belinda, we can't just disappear from the party."

"Yes, we can." Her arms tightened around his neck and she pressed herself closer against his chest. "We can just leave. We're newlyweds. Nobody will think it odd. Don't ruin things for Abby and Colette. Please, just take me home."

Her eyes were wide and her body shivered uncontrollably as she clung to him. Making up his mind, Derek carried her to his car and gently placed her inside. Junior hadn't been at the party because he'd been on duty. When they got back to Derek's house, he'd call the sheriff and Junior could take things from there.

It wasn't until they got back to Derek's and he'd turned on the living room lights, that he saw the extent of her injuries. Red and swollen, her neck was circled with angry marks beginning to bruise.

Rage swept through Derek. Rage that somebody had harmed what was his. Rage at himself for being stupid enough to let down his guard.

"Now tell me exactly what happened," he said as he sat next to her on the sofa.

She went through everything step by step, from the moment she'd walked out onto the porch to when Derek had found her slumped on the ground. As Derek heard the hoarseness of her voice, saw the abject fear that still darkened her eyes, his anger only increased.

"And you didn't recognize the voice?" he asked when she'd finished.

She shook her head, wincing as she brought a hand up to touch her throat. "No, and the bag came down over my head before I got a chance to see anyone." She closed her eyes, a hiccuping sob escaping from her lips. She looked at Derek once again. "All I know is that it was a man. The hands were too big, too strong, to be a woman's." Again a sob slipped from her lips. "Why is this happening, Derek? Why is this happening to me?"

He stroked the long silkiness of her hair in an effort to comfort her. "I don't know, sweetheart."

"Thank God you came out when you did. I—I think if you hadn't, I'd be dead."

"Shh, you're safe now." He pulled her into his arms and held her tight, felt the frantic pounding of her heart against his chest. Tenderness swept through him, protectiveness overwhelmed him. He wanted to swallow her whole, keep her inside him where she'd be safe until they figured out what monster was after her.

Reluctantly he released her and walked over to the telephone. "What are you doing?" she asked.

"We need to get Junior out here to talk to you." He picked up the receiver.

"No, Derek...please don't." She struggled to a sitting position. "I can't go through all the questions another time. And I don't know anything to help." Tears sparkled on the ends of her lashes, like diamonds framing her sapphire eyes. "I just want to take a bath and go to bed. Please."

He hesitated, then replaced the receiver in the cradle. She was right. There was little she could tell Junior that would help him catch the perpetrator and he had the feeling if pushed too hard, she'd break down all together.

"I'll go up and run a bath for you," he said. "Then while you're relaxing in the tub, I'll make us some hot tea, okay?"

She nodded and Derek went upstairs. Although since moving in the week before, Belinda had been using the guest bathroom, Derek ran a tubful of water in the Jacuzzi in the master bedroom. In here, the tub was deeper, larger and would be more comfortable for her.

It took him only minutes to fill the tub and add a splash of frothy bubbles. When it was ready, he went back downstairs, picked her up in his arms and carried her to where the bath awaited.

"I'll be downstairs in the kitchen," he said. "When you're finished, come on down." She nodded and he left the room, closing the door behind him.

Downstairs in the kitchen, Derek filled a teakettle with water and put it on to boil. From the drawer, he pulled out the list of suspects he and Belinda had been working on, then carried it to the table and sat.

He worked a hand through his hair in frustration as he thought of this latest attack. Dammit, he'd allowed his vigilance to wane. He should have kept her by his side every moment they'd been at the party.

But he'd believed they were safe, surrounded by friends and family. And now he knew for certain— one of their friends, somebody they trusted, wanted Belinda dead.

Why? The succinct word echoed in his head. Rarely was a crime committed without motive. What reason could anyone possibly possess to want Belinda dead?

And why, why did he know in his gut that it revolved around him, around the fire that had nearly killed him? Was it possible that somebody wanted to destroy him? What better way than to murder the woman he'd married?

He jumped as the teakettle whistled, sounding disturbingly like a high-pitched scream. He moved the kettle off the burner, then blew out a sigh of frustration. Although he'd agreed for Belinda's sake not to call Junior, he owed Abby and Colette a quick call to explain their mysterious absence.

Abby answered the call, and it was obvious from the noise that emanated in the background that the party was still going strong. "Abby, it's Derek."

"Hey, where'd you guys disappear to?"

"Belinda was getting tired and we decided to sneak out and come home."

Abby laughed. "Sure, I've heard that 'tired' excuse before. Did she have a good time?"

"I'm sure she'll never forget it," Derek said truthfully. "Anyway, I just wanted to give you a quick call and tell you thanks, and please thank everyone who came."

"Derek, I'm just so happy for both of you. It's so wonderful that you found each other again after all these years." He could hear the smile in her voice. "Now go," she exclaimed. "Go act like a newlywed and tell Belinda I'll talk to her tomorrow."

Go act like a newlywed. Abby's words rang in his ears as he said goodbye and hung up. There was nothing he'd like to do more than act like a newlywed.

From the moment Belinda had moved into the house as his wife, he'd been fighting his desire for her. She'd not only moved her clothes into the spare bedroom, but somehow had managed to imbibe the entire house with her presence.

He smelled her perfume when he awakened in the mornings, went to bed at night with dreams of her filling his head. He'd thought it would be easy, to have her in his home, share his life with her for however long was necessary, and not feel any hunger, any passion for her that he couldn't control.

However, over the course of the past week, he'd felt his hunger for her building, transforming into a need he wasn't sure could be controlled.

But of course, he would control it. He wouldn't break his agreement with Belinda that there would be no intimacy between them. To do so would be foolish, and would only make it more difficult when it came time for them to say their final goodbye to one another. And they would say goodbye. He knew the only reason Belinda had married him was to save her home, and when she'd fulfilled her end of that bargain, she'd move on.

He looked at the clock, wondering how much longer she would be. Pacing the length of the kitchen, he once again replayed those moments of literally stumbling across Belinda on the ground.

He assumed that when he'd stepped out onto the porch and called her name into the darkness of the night, he'd scared off her attacker. Had he paused a moment before calling to her, had he been stopped on his way out the back door by somebody, it would have been too late. This thought not only sobered him, it horrified him.

Once again he looked at the clock, becoming more and more concerned with each passing moment that Belinda didn't appear. Maybe he should go check on her, just to make certain she was all right. She'd not only had a terrifying scare, but she'd also suffered physically from the trauma.

He took the stairs two at a time, stopping in front of the closed bedroom door. He knocked. No answer. "Belinda?" He knocked again, louder this time. Still no answer.

"Belinda, are you okay?" When there was still no reply, he opened the door and stepped in. He saw her immediately, still in the tub. Only her head was visible above the layer of strawberry scented bubbles, and that was slumped back and to the side. She looked unconscious…or worse.

Had her throat swelled up, constricting her air? Had she suffered a head injury he hadn't been aware of? He should have never left her alone. He should have taken her directly to a hospital.

As he reached the side of the sunken tub, her eyelids fluttered, then opened. "Are you all right?" he asked, unsure whether to step closer or step away.

"I—I must have fallen asleep." She raised a hand and smoothed her water-slickened hair. Sitting up, she exposed her shoulders and the creamy swell of her breasts.

She gazed at him, her eyes a smoky blue. They seemed to be whispering to him, beckoning him closer, promising him pleasures that weakened his previous resolve.

His mouth suddenly felt unaccountably dry. He took a step backward. "I'll just get out of here and let you finish up."

"Don't go." She whispered the words as she rose out of the water.

Derek knew he should run like hell, but his feet refused to meet his brain's commands. Instead, he drank in the beauty of her nakedness as bubbles slid off to expose her inch by inch. He could smell the scent of strawberries, knew her skin would taste of them…knew he was in deep trouble.

"Belinda." He wasn't sure whether he meant her name as a protest or a plea.

She stepped out of the tub and moved toward him, trailing bubbles and creating a fire in the pit of his stomach he feared would consume him.

"Belinda…I don't think this is a good—" The rest of his words were halted as she placed a finger against his lips. Her scent surrounded him, clean… sweet…feminine.

"Don't tell me it's not a good idea. I don't want to hear reason. I don't want to be rational. I just want you to hold me, make love to me."

Before he could voice another protest, she reached up on tiptoes and pressed her mouth to his. The kiss tasted of hungry need and aggressive want, and as her tongue touched the tip of his, the flames of desire surged within him.

He stroked her back, the skin soft as velvet beneath his touch. As he reveled in the feel of her, her fingers worked to unfasten his shirt buttons.

As she pulled the shirt from his shoulders, her lips moved from his mouth to the hollow of his throat.

Someplace in the back of his head, some remnant of reason remained and he knew he should stop her...stop this, before they were in over their heads.

But, heaven help him, he didn't want to stop. As he felt her breasts pressing against his bare chest, heard the husky moan that growled deep in her throat, he let the last of his doubts fade away.

He picked her up and carried her to the bed, where he gently lay her down. He stood hesitantly by the edge of the bed, giving her a final opportunity to change her mind. She didn't. "Make love to me, Derek," she whispered urgently, reaching out to pluck impatiently at the button fly on his jeans.

He stepped away from her touch and instead crossed the room and turned off the ceiling light. Moonlight streamed in the window, dancing on Belinda's body, highlighting the pale gold of her drying hair.

He moved to the curtains and pulled them shut, plunging the room into complete darkness. He'd lost his rational, reasonable mind where she was concerned, but he hadn't forgotten to protect himself. He'd make love to her, but he'd do it in total darkness, where she couldn't see his scars.

BELINDA KNEW that making love with Derek would only make things more difficult between them. But the moment she'd opened her eyes and seen him standing by the bathtub, his gaze lit with fierce longing, she'd decided to hell with the consequences.

She'd tasted death tonight and now more than anything she wanted the energy of life to flow through her, the sweet swell of passion to banish all thoughts from her mind, all darkness from her soul.

She felt a moment's panic when he shut off all the lights and closed the curtains, plunging the room in the same kind of profound darkness that she'd slipped into with those strong hands around her throat. "Derek?"

"Shh. I'm right here." His voice came from just beside the bed.

She heard him unbutton his jeans, heard the whisper of denim as he slid them off. The bed depressed with his weight and he was beside her, his hands on her breasts as his lips captured hers.

Like the refrain from a half-forgotten favorite song, familiar, nearly forgotten sensations rushed through Belinda with each stroke of Derek's hands.

She arched her body to meet each caress, sighed her pleasure when his mouth moved to capture first one nipple, then the other. Hearing his ragged breathing only stoked the flames of her desire higher.

His broad back warmed her hands as she caressed the muscles and planes. The spicy, masculine scent of him intoxicated her, caused her senses to whirl with each intimate touch.

She lost track of time and space, forgot the past and future. The only emotion she could sustain beneath the onslaught of his lovemaking was a mind-bending passion.

When she could take it no more, when he'd touched every inch of her body and had her nerves screaming in tortured pleasure, she pushed him away. She wanted to touch him, explore all of him with the same intimacy he'd shown to her.

Running her hands down his chest, across the flat

of his stomach, she felt his swift intake of air then his low moan of excitement.

She gasped as he grabbed her hands, halting her exploration. Rolling her onto her back, he pulled her arms above her head, capturing her hands in a firm grasp. He moved his lower body between her legs and entered her at the same time his lips possessed hers.

Slowly at first, they moved together in perfect unison. As their bodies melded, their heartbeats conversed, beating together in the rhythm of desire.

She wrapped her legs around his back, urging him closer, deeper, and he accelerated his movements, building to a frenzy.

Tears pressed against her eyelids as she felt herself rushing closer and closer, spiraling higher and higher. As she reached the pinnacle and plunged over the edge, she cried out his name, felt him stiffen against her as he joined her in a delirious spin down to earth.

Almost immediately afterward, Derek moved out of their embrace and got up. She heard him fumble in the darkness, heard the rustle of his jeans. "Derek?" She sat and pushed her tangled hair away from her face. Her body still tingled with the afterglow of their lovemaking.

The overhead light blinked on, blinding her for a moment with its jarring glare. When her vision focused, she saw him standing by the doorway, his jeans on and a T-shirt in hand.

"I'm sorry, Belinda. That should have never happened."

The words, the coolness of his tone, shot through her like a knife piercing through her heart. "Please, don't say that."

"I have to say that," he returned angrily. "We made an agreement, and we broke it tonight. I don't want you to get any crazy ideas that somehow this meant anything to me."

Bitterness bubbled inside her. "What makes you think this meant anything to me?" she countered. "I needed somebody and you were convenient."

"Just so we understand each other."

"Trust me, I understand perfectly."

For a moment their gazes locked, and in his she saw distance, alienation and just a whisper of what looked to be pain.

"It won't happen again," he said, then turned and left the room.

Belinda shivered despite the warmth of the room as an aching regret surged through her. He was right. It had been an enormous mistake.

For a little while, as he'd kissed her, loved her, she'd been able to fool herself. She'd believed it wasn't just a momentary thing based on lust. While in the shelter of his arms, she'd managed to believe that somehow their hearts had found each other once again.

He was right. It would never happen again. She'd have to be declared mentally insane before she'd allow herself to be touched by Derek Walker again.

Chapter Twelve

"If you're going to be gone all day, then I'd like to spend the day with my sisters," Belinda told Derek as she met him in the kitchen. He was leaving on an early morning flight to get the children and bring them home. They'd both agreed that it would be best if he went alone so too many new things wouldn't be thrust on the kids all at the same time.

Clad in a navy three-piece suit and a crisp white shirt, Derek looked more like a successful businessman than a man going to collect his new family.

"Belinda, you know I don't think that's a good idea," he said as he measured coffee into the machine.

"I don't care whether you think it's a good idea or not," she countered. "I've been cooped up in this house for the last ten days. I need a break." A break away from him and his cool silences.

Since the night they'd made love, they'd circled each other warily, keeping their distance and being so polite it made Belinda's teeth grind.

He turned away from the coffee machine and looked at her, his brow wrinkled thoughtfully. "I suppose it wouldn't hurt for you to hang out with your sisters while I'm gone." The grimness of his features that she'd come to expect from him the past week softened somewhat. "I know it's been rough, Belinda, but you know what Junior said. The safest place for you right now is inside this house. Until we find out who's threatening you, you aren't safe anywhere else."

"And what if we never find out who's after me? I just spend the rest of my life like a prisoner here?"

"We'll find him," Derek replied firmly.

"How? We're no closer now than we were after the first attempt on my life." Frustration made her voice more snappish than she'd intended. "I'm sorry, I'm taking it out on you and it isn't your fault. I'm just discouraged." She sank into a chair at the table. "Somebody is playing games with my life and not only is it frightening me, it's starting to really make me angry."

"I feel the same way," he acknowledged. He leaned against the counter, his gaze lingering on her. "You won't wander off alone?"

She shook her head, a hand reaching up to touch her throat where the bruises had faded but a lingering soreness remained. "Trust me, I have a very clear memory of what happened the last time I wandered off alone."

"I'll drop you off on my way to the airport, then pick you up as we come back late this evening." He turned back to the counter and poured them each a cup of coffee. "I'm still worried about bringing the kids here right now," he said as he placed a cup in front of her, then joined her at the table.

"But we agreed that postponing their arrival might weigh poorly in the judge's eyes. Besides, nobody has tried to harm Cody." She paused a moment to sip her coffee, grateful for the warmth of the brew, then continued. "Let's face it, Derek. The target is me. Nobody else."

They drank their coffee in silence, the same stifling silence that had shouted between them since the night they'd made love.

For Belinda, that particular night had taken on the dimensions of a dream. First, the viciousness of the attack, leaving her shaken and terrified. Then, the utter abandon of making love to Derek, also leaving her shaken and terrified, although in an entirely different way.

For the past several days the easiest way to handle it all was to pretend that none of it had happened. Forget the feel of malevolent hands around her throat. Forget the sensation of Derek's fingers stroking heat throughout her body.

But now, memories of Derek's touch winged through her. She'd hoped that her memory of their lovemaking three years before had been enhanced by the passage of time. Someplace deep within her she'd believed there was no way possible that it had been as wonderful, as breathtaking, as she'd remembered.

She'd been wrong. Her memory hadn't exaggerated or embellished. Making love with Derek was just as magnificent, just as powerful, as she remembered. And all she wanted to do was forget the entire experience. As he apparently had.

Finishing her coffee, she stood and took her cup to the dishwasher. "I'll just run upstairs and get ready."

He looked at his watch. "We need to leave here in the next fifteen minutes."

She nodded and went upstairs to the master suite. She'd moved all her clothes in here before going down for coffee. With the children arriving later today, starting tonight she'd be staying in the master suite with Derek.

As her fingers nimbly braided the length of her hair, she eyed the king-size bed with trepidation. Surely it was big enough that sleeping with Derek would be no different than sleeping alone. They were both adults, both in agreement of what this marriage would entail. Sleeping with him should be no problem at all.

Still, her stomach quivered nervously as she thought of lying next to him in the dark, feeling his body heat next to her. Stop it, she commanded herself irritably.

She grabbed one of her sweaters from the closet and pulled it on over her T-shirt. The red turtleneck would hide any remaining black and blue on her neck from her sisters.

Before heading down the stairs, she checked first in Tasha's room, then Toby's to make certain all was ready for them. She paused in Toby's doorway, as always the room creating a wistful, aching pain in her heart.

If only Derek had loved her enough. If only she hadn't run to Kansas City, pregnant and so alone. She closed her eyes, allowing herself to remember for a moment. The pain. The blood. All alone and so scared. All alone when she'd delivered. If only Derek had loved her enough to want her, then perhaps the tragedy wouldn't have happened.

She turned away from the bedroom, surprised that for the first time she didn't feel the black bitterness directed toward Derek. For the first time she realized it was difficult to hold him responsible for something he hadn't known. And would never know.

Her heartache over the lost little baby boy was her own and she selfishly guarded it, mourning him silently, too deeply for words. Telling Derek about the baby would change nothing.

Walking down the stairs, she realized how much she was looking forward to spending the day with Abby and Colette. Although she'd spoken on the phone to them nearly every day, she hadn't seen either one of them since the night of the party. She needed a day of girl talk and laughter, a day spent with her sisters.

"All set?" Derek picked up a briefcase Belinda knew was stuffed full of legal papers pertaining to the children's case. She grabbed a jacket from the coat closet, then together they walked out of the house and to his car.

"You promise me you'll be careful today," he said moments later as they pulled up in front of the Connor ranch house. "Don't go anywhere isolated. Stay where there are several people. Don't allow yourself to be alone with anyone except your sisters."

Belinda held up a hand to halt his litany of admonitions. "I promise all of the above." She turned to open her door but halted as he placed a hand on her arm. She looked back at him and he leaned toward her and placed his lips on hers.

The kiss was soft, sweet, lacking the intensity of their previous kisses yet touching her with its tenderness. As he pulled back, he grazed her cheek with a fleeting caress. "We'll see you tonight."

Belinda nodded and stumbled from the car, confused by the mixed signals he sent her, disturbed by the immediate want his sweet touch evoked inside her.

When she saw Abby standing in the doorway, her confusion melted away, replaced by a surge of bitter understanding. Of course, that's why he'd kissed her. He'd seen Abby standing there and had played his part of loving husband.

"Hey, what a pleasant surprise." Abby greeted her with a hug.

"I hope you don't mind. Derek is going to be gone all day. He's flying out to pick up the children, so I thought I'd spend the day here," Belinda explained.

"Mind? I'm delighted. We haven't seen enough of you since you and Derek got married." Together the two women went inside, where the rest of the family was at the kitchen table eating breakfast.

As always, breakfast at the Connors' was served with plenty of talk and laughter. This morning, there was no talk of losing the ranch, no worried frowns to mar the liveliness of the conversation. Instead the talk was filled with plans for the future.

"I talked to Charlie Rippert about buying enough grain to get the cattle through the winter," Luke said.

"Good. Come spring we'll plant some new crops and hopefully next year we won't have to buy grain from anyone else," Abby replied.

Dreams and hopes filled the air, and any doubts Belinda had entertained about her marriage to Derek disappeared. Somehow, some way, she'd fulfill her end of the bargain to him, as he'd already fulfilled his to her.

After breakfast, the three sisters cleaned the dishes while the men disappeared for morning chores. "I swear, Belinda. Marriage to Derek seems to agree with you. You have that glow all newlyweds wear," Colette said as she handed Belinda another dish to rinse.

Belinda smiled self-consciously. "The glow you're talking about is probably due to eating too many of Abby's pancakes."

"Belinda's newlywed status is about to be adjusted. By this evening she'll be a newlywed mother," Abby reminded Colette.

"Oh, that's right." Colette's eyes sparkled. "Six months ago who would have thought we'd all be happily married and raising families of our own?"

"I wish Mom and Dad were here to see us now," Abby said softly.

"Me, too," Belinda agreed.

For a moment grief hung between the three, a shared grief that only strengthened the bonds of sisterhood between them.

Belinda took Abby's hand, then Colette's, in hers. "You know, when Roger first told us about his father and the fact that one of us might be his half-sister, it frightened me. I didn't want to think about the fact that one of us is adopted. I was so afraid that if we found out who it was, things would change between us." Belinda squeezed her sisters' hands. "I'm not afraid anymore. I realize now it doesn't matter what's written on a piece of paper. You are my sisters in my heart, and nobody can ever take that away from me.''

Somehow the three of them were in each other's arms, laughing and hugging and more than a little teary-eyed. "It's a moot point anyway," Abby said with a final hug to Belinda and Colette. "Apparently Mom didn't want us to find those adoption papers, because I've ransacked this house and they're nowhere to be found.''

Belinda smiled. "Mom always was the best at hiding things. Remember our Easter egg hunts? There were always eggs we couldn't find because she was so creative in hiding them.''

"I can't help but feel sorry for Roger. All he wants is to grant his father's greatest wish before he dies," Colette said as she sank into a chair at the table.

"Yes, but what can we do about it? Without those papers we don't have a clue which one of us might be Roger's half-sister," Belinda replied. She turned to Abby. "You're the oldest. Do you have any memory of Mom being pregnant? Do you remember me or Colette being born?''

"I would have been two when you came, three when Colette was born.'' Abby shook her head. "I just don't have any memories that early in my life.''

Brook yelled from her high chair, demanding her mother's attention. "Okay, my sticky little sweetheart, I'll get you out of that chair," Colette said to her daughter. Brook clapped her hands together and gave them all a toothless grin.

"I'll clean her up," Belinda offered. She picked up the six-month old and kissed her chubby little cheek.

"Come on, Aunt Belinda will wash that syrup off you."

It took Belinda only a few minutes to clean up Brook and change her clothes. As she carried Brook back to Colette, she breathed in her baby scent.

Would she someday have a real marriage to a man she loved? Would she one day get the opportunity to have another baby, one she could hold and love, watch grow?

"Thanks, Belinda," Colette said as Belinda returned Brook. Colette smiled at her daughter. "Want to go watch Daddy get thrown off a horse?" She looked at Belinda. "Hank is breaking one of the Hortons' horses. He's been working with the horse for the past couple of weeks and is going to try to ride it this morning. Want to come watch?"

"Sure."

After bundling up in jackets, they stepped out into the cool morning. Already a crowd had gathered around the corral. Abby and Cody were there, Cody dancing in excitement as he announced that his Uncle Hank was the "bestest horse rider in the world."

Belinda found herself studying the workers who'd taken a break from chores to watch the action about to take place. Had one of them broken into the house and attempted to stab her? Was one of them responsible for nearly choking her to death?

Billy Sims stood off by himself, his usual scowl creasing his broad forehead. Bulldog and Philip Weiss leaned against the fence, Bulldog's face rapt as Philip more than likely spun a tale of adventure from his youthful days.

"Good morning, Belinda. Come to watch the

fun?'' Roger slipped up beside her, his hat covering his blond hair.

"Hi, Roger. Yeah, I decided I needed a visit home for the day.''

"Married life treating you okay?''

"Fine,'' she replied smoothly. "I understand you're seeing my best friend.''

Roger's thin mustache danced upward with his grin and he swept his hat off. "Janice is terrific. We have a great time together. You two known each other for long?''

Belinda shook her head. "Only for about six months. We met in a dental office and things just clicked between us.''

He studied her face for a long moment. "You know, you look like her. Something about your eyes...the structure of your face.''

"I look like Janice?'' she asked in confusion.

He shook his head and smiled. "No, not Janice. Marie...my father's mistress.''

"Did you know her?''

Roger shook his head. "Not well. I met her a few times but had no idea of her relationship with my father.'' He looked to where Hank led a huge white horse out of the barn. "She was quite beautiful. You, more than your sisters, remind me of her.''

Belinda found his comment oddly disconcerting. "How is your father doing?''

Roger's pleasant features pulled into a frown. "Not well. I'm in touch daily with his personal physician. I just wish you-all could find those adoption papers. I still hope to give my father the final gift of his daughter before he passes on.''

"I'm sorry we haven't been able to help you. We've looked everywhere for those papers."

"I'm hoping they'll turn up before it's too late." He studied her once again. "Would you agree to a DNA test?"

She looked at him in surprise. "Sure, I guess I would." She no longer feared discovering which of them had been adopted, knew in her heart nothing could ever change her love for the two women she called sisters.

"Good, I'll talk to Abby and Colette to see if they'll agree to the test." He looked relieved and Belinda's heart went out to him. He apparently loved his father very much.

She touched his arm lightly. "I'm sure Abby and Colette will do anything they can to help you."

"I don't want to mess up anyone's life," he hurriedly added. "I just know what a comfort it would be to my father to be able to look at, perhaps hug, the daughter he never got to father."

"Your father is lucky to have a son like you."

Roger blushed and slapped his hat on his head. "I've tried to be a good son, although I'm sure my dad would agree I haven't always succeeded."

"We all have times when we disappoint our parents," Belinda replied.

They both turned their attention to the corral, where Hank had mounted the white horse. Whoops and hollers resounded as the horse shied then bucked, trying to dislodge the unfamiliar weight of the rider.

Belinda watched her brother-in-law, admiring the picture he made on the back of the horse. Funny how both Abby and Colette had married men who physically looked a lot alike. Black hair and shadowed eyes, they were handsome men, if you liked that kind of dark attractiveness.

While on one level Belinda found them good-looking, on a deeper level, they did absolutely nothing for her. Her dream lover had sun-kissed hair and warm brown eyes. She frowned irritably as she realized whenever she fantasized about the man of her dreams, his face was always Derek's.

The diamond ring he'd placed on her finger sparkled in the sunshine. At some point in the future she would give it back to him and their pretend marriage would be over. The Connor ranch would be safe, Derek would have his children, and everyone would be happy.

As she thought of the way he'd reacted after they'd made love, the ensuing silence and coolness directed toward her, she told herself the end of her marriage couldn't come a day too soon.

DEREK DROVE the distance from the airport to the Connor ranch with the radio off, the only sound in the car the soft, rhythmic breathing of the sleeping children in the back seat.

The trip had gone without a hitch. The children had been thrilled to see him, had clung to him with eager excitement during the transfer procedure from the foster home into his care.

Having the kids in his custody was a curious blend of happiness and grief. His brother and sister-in-law should be alive, raising their children and growing old together. But a drunk driver had ended their life and now it would be Derek watching the children grow up.

As he neared the Connor ranch, thoughts of Belinda filled his head. Making love to her had been a mistake. It had merely served to whet his appetite for more and that was an appetite he didn't intend to indulge ever again.

He'd managed to manipulate their lovemaking so it happened under safe conditions...under the cover of darkness. He'd also made sure she didn't touch him too intimately, didn't explore the length of his body. He couldn't guarantee that if they made love again, the same conditions would prevail.

Better he keep her at arm's length, not only physically but emotionally, as well. He tightened his grip on the steering wheel, knowing the difficulty he faced.

Initially, when he'd first come up with the marriage scheme, he'd thought it would be easy to keep his distance from her. After all, he'd believed she'd turned her back on him, diminished what he'd believed they'd shared in the past. Now he knew she hadn't done that, that his mother hadn't told her how to contact him.

The edge of bitterness he'd planned on using as a defense was gone, and that only made things more difficult for him.

Something else complicating the entire situation was the danger to Belinda. Because of the threats and attacks that had already occurred, Derek was reluctant to leave her alone for any length of time.

In this case, familiarity was not breeding contempt, rather it was intensifying a slow burn of desire inside him. He awakened each morning wanting her, and went to bed at night with the same hungry need.

And starting tonight she'd be sleeping in his bed. He groaned aloud as he thought of lying next to her, breathing her sweet scent all night long and not touching her, not holding her.

As he pulled up in front of the Connor house, he asked himself when it had happened. When in the hell had he fallen back in love with Belinda?

Chapter Thirteen

Belinda would have had to possess a heart of stone not to fall instantly in love with Tasha and Toby. Although they were still asleep when Derek arrived to pick her up, Belinda and Derek awakened them when they arrived at Derek's house.

It took nearly an hour for them to get the children unpacked and settled in their rooms, then the four of them had cookies and milk at the kitchen table.

Toby was quiet, seeming quite satisfied to allow his older sister to monopolize the conversation. But each time Belinda's gaze caught his, he gifted her with a shy, sweet smile.

Tasha chattered like a magpie, describing to Belinda their foster home, the airplane ride and her happiness to be with her uncle Derek.

Belinda found both of the children utterly enchanting. She understood Derek's obsessive need to make certain he gained custody. He'd be a good father to them. This thought brought a blossom of pain to her as she remembered the child he'd never get a chance to father, a child she'd never get a chance to mother.

By nine o'clock Toby's and Tasha's eyelids

drooped with sleepiness and Belinda and Derek took the two to bed. Toby was asleep the moment his head touched the pillow. Derek gave Tasha a kiss good-night, then went downstairs, leaving Belinda and the little girl alone in the frilly, feminine bedroom.

Belinda leaned down and kissed Tasha's forehead. "Good night, sweetie." She turned to leave but Tasha caught her hand.

"My mommy and daddy are in heaven."

Belinda sat on the edge of the bed and smoothed a strand of blond hair away from Tasha's cherubic little face. "I know," she answered softly, her heart aching for the child.

"I'm glad we're going to live here with you and Uncle Derek. Uncle Derek said Mommy and Daddy would want us here." Her brown eyes, so like Derek's, blinked with sleepiness.

"I'm glad you're going to live here, too."

Tasha yawned and snuggled beneath the covers, her hand still gripping Belinda's. "Now I've got an angel mommy and you. I'm glad you're going to be my mommy here." The little girl's eyes fluttered closed and within moments her fingers had relaxed their hold on Belinda's.

Belinda stood, her heart full of emotion. She walked to the doorway and paused a moment to look at the sleeping child.

Neither she nor Derek had considered the conse-quences of her parenting the kids for a year, then walking out of their lives. She hadn't considered the possibility that she'd fall in love with the children.

Oh, the kids would survive when she left. Children were resilient and they would adjust to her absence.

But already, after only a couple of hours, they had burrowed into her heart. It was as if Fate had conspired to make walking away as difficult as possible.

She left the bedroom and went in search of Derek. She didn't want to think about leaving right now, refused to contemplate the heartache that she'd eventually suffer.

She found Derek on the porch swing. "They both asleep?" he asked as she stepped out onto the front porch.

"Yes." He moved over to give her room to sit beside him. "They're great kids."

"Yeah, they are," he agreed. "Mike and Marilyn did a good job, for what time they had." His voice thickened. "I just wish they'd had more time."

Belinda knew no words she could utter would distill his grief over his brother and sister-in-law's untimely deaths. Instead of saying anything, she touched the back of his hand.

He cleared his throat and sat up straighter, causing the swing to sway. "How was your day with your sisters?"

"Nice. It was fun seeing them both filled with such hope for the future." She gazed at him, the moonlight stroking his bold features. "We have you to thank for that."

He smiled. "Your sister sent me a report, kind of a prospectus on what they intend to do with the money I invested. She has some good ideas."

"Abby's always had good ideas, just never enough money to implement them."

For a moment they sat silent, the sounds of night surrounding them. Their silence wasn't forced or strained, but rather natural, peaceful. The swing swayed to and fro, relaxing Belinda with its gentle movement.

It was easy to forget for a moment that their marriage had been nothing but a business deal. Easy to forget the past and pretend they were two parents sharing a moment of togetherness at the end of a busy day.

A fool's pretense. She couldn't allow herself to get caught up in the illusion they presented to the outside world. Reality was that their marriage was a business deal, that Derek had no intention of it being anything other than that. He'd been quite clear that he wanted no emotional investment.

"Roger asked if I'd agree to a DNA test today," she said, breaking the silence and pulling her thoughts away from the state of her marriage.

"What did you tell him?"

Belinda shrugged. "I told him I'd do it. Since Junior checked him out and we know he's exactly who he says he is and his story seems to be true, I see no reason not to try to accommodate him."

"Will it bother you if you find out you were adopted?"

"Up until a couple of months ago I would have said yes." She leaned back in the swing, conscious of his arm just behind her. "The idea that I might not really belong terrified me. Somehow in the last month or so, I've realized that it has nothing to do with belonging. I belong here, and my sisters will always be my family. Family is a state of mind, not a state of birth."

"I hope Toby and Tasha feel that way one day."

"They will. All it takes is love, and it's obvious you love them."

He nodded. "I do. They're all the family I'll ever have."

"Surely someday you'll have your own children," she said, ignoring the catch in her heart.

"No. I don't intend to have children." He looked away from her and directed his gaze toward the moon in the distance. "Once we've divorced, I don't intend to marry again."

Belinda studied him, wondering what had happened to the dreams he'd shared with her so long ago...dreams of marriage and family.

What had made him change? What had destroyed those dreams he'd once had? As she watched, he rubbed his thigh, as if kneading out some deep pain.

"What happened to your leg, Derek?"

He looked down, as if surprised to see his hand massaging it. "I broke it a couple years ago. The doctors had to put a pin in."

"It must have been a bad break."

"It was."

She wanted to ask him more...exactly how he'd broken it. She wanted to know what he'd been doing in the years since he'd left here. Had he fallen in love? Had his heart been broken? Had he ever thought of her? The questions burned inside her, but refused to be verbalized.

He stood. "We'd better get to bed. I imagine the kids will be up early."

Bed. In Derek's bed. A curious mixture of emotions surged through Belinda as she watched him lock the front door, set the security code, then start up the stairs to his room.

"I'm going to get a drink of water. I'll be up in just a minute," she explained.

Filling a glass with water, Belinda felt a curious mixture of dread mingling with taunting heat racing through her body as she thought of sleeping next to Derek.

Funny, in all their history together, they'd never slept together. Whenever, wherever they'd made love, Belinda had always gone home when their passion was spent.

She took a sip of the cool water, her thoughts racing back in time. On the night of the fire, Belinda had planned to spend the night with Derek. His parents were to be gone all night and they'd planned on being together, falling asleep and awakening in each other's arms.

Belinda had chickened out, afraid Derek's parents might come home earlier than planned, afraid of being caught in an indelicate position.

Her heart skipped a beat as a new thought intruded. Was it possible the fire had never been intended to harm Derek or his family? Was it possible she'd been the target all along?

She slammed her glass down and raced up the stairs to the master suite. She skidded to a stop as she saw Derek, already in bed, the sheets at his waist, exposing the tanned expanse of his muscular chest.

A lamp on the bedside stand was the only illumination, its soft glow creating an intimacy that weakened Belinda's knees.

The thought that had propelled her up the stairs fled her mind. All she wanted to do was curl up next to his chest, feel the beating of his heart against her own, lose herself in the heat of his body.

"You coming to bed or do you intend to stand there for the remainder of the night?"

His terseness snapped her inertia. "Derek, I just thought of something. It might be important." She sat on the end of the bed as he sat up. She averted her gaze, unable to look at him and keep her thoughts straight. "Remember the night of the fire?"

"You might say that night is burned into my memory," he said wryly.

"Well, do you remember that I was going to spend the night with you? We'd talked about it, planned it. I'd told Abby and Colette I was going to spend the night with a girlfriend in town, it was all set, then I chickened out."

"Is there a point to this little sojourn into the past?"

"Yes, there's a point," Belinda replied, refocusing her gaze on him. "I was supposed to be in that house that night. What if the fire that was set, wasn't set to hurt you or your family, but was set in an effort to hurt me?"

He didn't answer. He didn't move, but she could tell by his expression that he was thinking about what she'd said.

After a moment of reflection, he shook his head. "It doesn't make sense. That somebody would burn my house down to hurt you. How would anyone know you planned to be in the house? It just doesn't make sense."

Belinda stood and began to pace back and forth at the foot of the bed. "Of course it doesn't make sense.

None of this makes any sense. Why would somebody try to stab me? Strangle me?''

Derek raked a hand through his hair. ''Belinda, think about it. The fire took place over three years ago. What you're saying is that somebody has been trying to kill you for three years. You're either talking about a very patient killer or an inept one.''

Belinda sighed and sank onto the bed once again. ''But I left soon after the fire, and I didn't come back until five months ago. The killer wouldn't have had a chance to kill me since I wasn't here.'' She shivered, the thought of somebody hating her for so long frightening her.

''Belinda, come to bed,'' Derek said softly. ''It's been a long day. We can talk about this in the morning.''

She nodded and went into the bathroom to change into her nightgown. Her fingers shook as she pulled the silk gown over her head. A tremor raced through her as she unbraided her hair and brushed its length. Her stomach clenched and unclenched as she turned off the bathroom light.

As she stepped back into the bedroom and eyed her side of the king-size bed, she tried to figure out if her fear was generated by the conversation they'd just had, or whether it had been created by the prospect of sleeping next to Derek. Two different kinds of fears, but one as real as the other.

Drawing a deep breath, she crossed the room and slid beneath the bed covers. She remained stiff, afraid to move, long after Derek had turned off the lamp and mumbled good-night.

Just one touch. She knew that's all it would take

from him. Just a single touch and she'd be in his arms. Despite the fact that she'd told herself making love to him was the last thing she wanted, she realized now it was the only thing she wanted.

Within minutes she heard the sound of Derek's deep, rhythmic breathing and knew he was asleep. Yes, making love to Derek was the only thing she wanted...and it seemed to be the last thing he wanted. Trying to ignore the press of hot tears against her eyelids, she turned so her back was to him and tried to sleep.

FOR THE THIRD MORNING in a row, Belinda awoke with Derek's body pressed tight against her back, his arm thrown across her shoulder as if in sleep he claimed her as his own. For the third morning in a row, she fought back tears as she slid from beneath his arm and got up.

It was early. Dawn was just beginning to chase the night shadows from the sky. She dressed quietly, then went downstairs to the kitchen to start the coffee.

Minutes later she sat at the table, listening to the silence of the early morning. It wouldn't be silent for long. For the past three days the house had been filled with the sounds of childish laughter. It was only at night after they'd gone to bed, and in the early morning hours before they awakened that silence reigned.

The children seemed to be adjusting well to their new lives. They adored Derek, who'd spent much of the past three days with them, and they seemed to adore Belinda, as well. They were loving children, eager for hugs and kisses and cuddly as teddy bears.

Fate had taken one baby from her, but had given

her two loving, needy children in return. Two children she would also have to tell goodbye.

And then there was Derek. During the day he was friendly with her, but with a reserved distance she couldn't breach. Only in his unguarded moments did she feel his gaze lingering on her. And only in sleep did he allow himself to touch her at all.

She loved him. Still. Always. Probably forever. She now realized loving Derek was as natural for her as breathing. She'd thought she hated him, had partially blamed him for the death of their child, but she now realized those emotions had been her shield, her feeble attempt to stop loving him.

Eventually she'd learn to live without him, knew he could never love her with the same intensity, the same longevity, that she loved him. She was resigned to the fact that once the adoption was finalized, she no longer had a place in his life, in his heart. But being resigned didn't make it easier.

"Good morning," Derek said as he entered the kitchen.

"Morning." Belinda averted her gaze, afraid her feelings for him would be apparent in her eyes. She'd already lost her heart to him, her very soul…the only thing she had left was her pride, and she intended to hang on to that.

He poured himself a cup of coffee, then stood by the window and peered out, sipping thoughtfully from his mug. "Every morning the trees are more bare. Before long we'll wake up to snow." He turned and smiled at her. "The kids will love it."

She couldn't help but smile at the image of the two children and Derek playing in the snow. "I loved the snow when I was young. My sisters and I always built a snow princess by the base of the dragon tree.''

He joined her at the table, his features warm and relaxed. "What's a snow princess?"

"A snowman, but instead of a top hat and gloves, ours had an old lace curtain dress, string mop hair and a crown of aluminum foil.'' Belinda laughed at the memory. "She wasn't the most attractive princess in the world.''

"I thought we'd all drive into town this morning and do some shopping. The kids need new coats.''

"Derek, I can't. Janice called yesterday and I invited her for coffee this morning. I know you'd planned to work this afternoon. You and the kids go ahead and go this morning.''

"You know I don't like leaving you here alone.''

Belinda smiled reassuringly. "With the security system you know I'm safe, and Janice is certainly no threat to me.'' He looked dubious. "Please, Derek. I'll be fine, and the kids need those coats.''

"We'll only be gone an hour and a half, two at the most.''

"That will give me time for some girl talk with Janice, then I'll have lunch ready for you when you get back.'' Belinda looked out the window where the sun had crawled up high in the sky, portending a gorgeous late autumn day. "If it's warm enough, maybe I'll plan a picnic. The kids would like that and we won't have too many nice days left.''

She looked back at him. "Maybe it's over, Derek. It's been almost two weeks since anything has happened. Maybe whoever was after me has moved on, gone away...''

"Belinda, that's a dangerous thought to entertain." He reached out and covered her hand with his. "You can't let your guard down. You can't fool yourself into thinking this is all over. Whoever it is, is out there, waiting for an opportunity. We can't let him get that opportunity."

At some point as he talked, his hand began caressing hers and when he finished speaking, their gazes locked. In the depths of his eyes, Belinda saw concern and beneath that something stronger—the flicker of desire.

It both enticed and confused her. For the past week he'd been sending her mixed signals, keeping his physical distance yet speaking to her with his eyes. This morning, she was simply too vulnerable to deal with him. She pulled her hand away from his. "Don't worry, I don't intend to let down my guard." *Not only my guard against whoever is trying to kill me, but also my guard against you,* she added silently.

She was grateful nearly two hours later when Derek and the kids left the house for their trip into town. She needed some time alone. Time to think. Time to assess.

There were times she thought she saw something akin to caring in Derek's eyes. Times she saw flashes of the younger man who'd vowed his undying love for her. But those flashes were all too brief, usually making her wonder if she'd only imagined the expression she longed to see.

As she made their bed and straightened their room, she thought of those moments of sleep, when he invariably sought the closeness of her body. Would he do the same if she were anyone else?

She stood for a moment in the doorway of Toby's room, waiting for a surge of angry grief to sweep over her, needing those old emotions to keep her safe from loving Derek. As she thought of the baby she'd lost, she felt grief...but no anger. Her shield of bitterness toward Derek was gone.

Back in the kitchen, she began to pack their picnic lunch. She'd just finished and set it on the counter when she heard the sound of the doorbell. Good. She'd rather lose herself in silly gossip with Janice than think about the futility of loving Derek.

"Hey, girl." Janice greeted her with a big hug. "It seems like it's been forever since I've seen you. You've become a recluse since your marriage."

"We've just been really busy," Belinda replied as she led her friend to the kitchen. "Derek's niece and nephew arrived a few days ago and we've all been adjusting." She motioned Janice into a chair at the table and poured them each a cup of coffee.

"Oh, yeah, I heard something about that in town. So, where are the little rug rats now?"

"They went with Derek into town a little while ago."

"How do you like being a mommy?"

Belinda smiled. "They're terrific kids, so easy to love." To her horror, tears burned hot behind her eyes as emotion lodged in her throat.

"Hey, what's wrong?" Janice asked sympathetically.

Belinda closed her eyes, swallowing hard in an attempt to gain control. "Oh, Janice, things are so messed up." She looked at her friend, misery sweeping over her.

"What's messed up? Honey, tell me what's wrong."

Belinda took a deep breath, then told her friend about the terms of her marriage to Derek. When she finished, Janice grinned at her in admiration. "Wow, I would have never guessed you the type to marry a man for money alone. What do your sisters think about it?"

"They don't know, and I don't want them to know." Belinda sighed and twisted the diamond ring on her finger. "Besides, I know now I didn't marry Derek to save the ranch. I didn't marry him for his money, although that's what I told myself at the time."

"So why'd you marry him?"

"Because I love him. Because I never stopped loving him." Cathartic relief flowed through her as she spoke the words out loud. Still, another secret weighed heavy in her heart, needing to be told to somebody, shared with a friend. "I had his baby."

"What?" Janice nearly dropped her mug.

"I had Derek's baby." Again tears formed, and this time Belinda let them slide from her eyes, heating her cheeks as they formed a path. "About three weeks after the fire at Derek's place, I realized I was pregnant. I hadn't heard from him...not a word. I was scared and didn't know what to do."

"Is that why you moved to Kansas City?"

Belinda nodded. "I finally got a letter from Derek, a kiss-off note, and the next day I packed up and left town." She wiped at her tears. "I got a job with a marketing firm and rented a small apartment. The pregnancy went without any problems. I was young and healthy and the doctor felt confident I'd have no problems.'' She paused a moment, taking another deep breath. ''Still, I was so scared, and so alone. My labor came early. It hit hard and fast and without warning. I didn't have a phone, and the one woman who'd become my friend and who checked on me occasionally had gone out for the evening.''

Belinda twisted her wedding ring more frantically as memories of that horrible night tumbled around in her head. ''I delivered there in the apartment, all alone, and the baby was stillborn. A baby boy. That's when I decided I hated Derek, and I thought my hatred would keep me safe from ever loving him again. But it hasn't.''

''Does Derek know about the baby?''

Belinda shook her head. ''No. I've never told him. What difference does it make now? It's over, it's done, and nothing can change the past.''

''So what are you going to do now?''

Belinda rolled the question around in her mind as she stared down at the ring on her finger. ''I'm going to fight for him.'' The moment the words were out of her mouth, she knew the rightness of them. ''I don't want this to be a temporary marriage. I want Derek forever. He loved me once. Despite the letter he wrote me, I know he loved me years ago. I'm going to make him love me again.'' For the first time in weeks Belinda felt completely at peace.

She would fight for Derek's love, fight to remain a part of his life and the lives of Toby and Tasha. If she won, she'd spend the rest of her life with them. If she lost... She didn't even want to consider that possibility.

Chapter Fourteen

"Ah, perfect timing," Belinda said as Derek and the kids came through the front door. She set the picnic basket she'd filled next to the door.

"Aunt Belinda, we got new coats," Tasha exclaimed with childish excitement. "Mine is red and has a furry collar. See?" She pulled the new garment from a shopping bag.

"My, that's the prettiest coat I've ever seen," Belinda said, then turned to Toby. "Did you get a red coat and a fur collar, too?"

He giggled and shook his head. "I got a blue coat and we got mittens and boots."

"They're all ready for the winter snows," Derek said.

"And when it snows Uncle Derek says we can go out and play in it," Tasha said.

"We'll make snowballs and put them down Uncle Derek's back." The kids laughed at Belinda's suggestion, and Derek's lips curled up in a grin.

"We'll see who gets snow down their back when the time comes. Maybe it will be...Tasha." He grabbed the little girl and tickled her. "Or Toby." Toby squealed as Derek tickled him.

"Oh, no…" Belinda laughed and backed up as Derek advanced on her. She grabbed the picnic basket as a shield. "You don't want to ruin our lunch."

Derek laughed. "Okay. You win…this round."

"Are we going on a picnic?" Tasha asked as she eyed the basket. "Hurray, a picnic," she exclaimed happily as Belinda nodded.

"Just let me get a jacket." Belinda handed Derek the basket and a folded blanket, then grabbed her coat from the closet.

It was a perfect Indian summer day. The air held a remnant scent of late summer flowers tinged with the hint of winter's approach. The sun warmed their backs, tempered by a cool breeze. They walked some distance from the house, stopping along the way when the kids spied something interesting to explore.

Belinda allowed all doubts and fears to fall away, deciding simply to enjoy the moment with Derek and the children.

They found a spot in a shady clearing amid a grove of trees and spread out the blanket. Within minutes they were eating the lunch Belinda had prepared.

"I love peanut butter and jelly," Tasha said as she ate her sandwich.

"I hate peanut butter," Derek replied.

Belinda smiled. "That's why you have ham sandwiches."

"I don't know how anyone could hate peanut butter." Tasha shook her head, as if finding the idea inconceivable.

"When I was younger, your daddy used to chase

me around with a glob of peanut butter on a spoon. He'd try to catch me and make me eat it,'' Derek told the kids, who giggled at the story.

Belinda saw the darkness of grief that deepened the brown of Derek's eyes as he spoke of the brother he'd lost. She touched his arm, wanting him to know she saw it, recognized it and empathized.

He smiled at her and the darkness in his eyes lifted. In that moment, more than ever before, she felt like his wife, his life partner, his support.

"This was a great idea," he said later as he stretched out on the blanket. He lay on his back, his arms folded beneath his head. They'd finished eating and the kids were playing catch with a ball Belinda had packed. They'd all shrugged out of their coats as the afternoon sun grew warmer.

"It was, wasn't it." Belinda moved the basket aside and joined him on the blanket, stretching out on her side to face him.

He looked more relaxed, more at ease than she'd ever seen him. He smelled of sunshine and fresh air and she longed to move closer, to touch the lines on his face, taste his lips with hers.

Her love for him rose up inside her, tingled in every fiber of her being, filled her with a restless energy she didn't know how to contain.

How many days had they spent on a blanket when they were younger? How many nights? A blanket had been their bedroom in that summer of heat they'd shared.

"Are there any grapes left?" he asked, breaking into her memories.

Belinda nodded, straightened and reached for the

basket, relieved for any activity. She withdrew the bag of plump purple grapes, then resumed her position, only this time closer to him.

She pulled one of the grapes out of the bag and held it to his lips, acutely conscious of her breast brushing his side, her leg pressed against his.

His eyes narrowed as his mouth plucked the grape from her fingers. She readied another piece of the fruit and held it out to him. "What are you doing, Belinda?" he asked softly.

She felt a blush steal over her face. "What do you mean? I'm just feeding my husband some fruit."

He took the grape from her and chewed thoughtfully, his gaze still warming her face. "No. You're playing with fire and I think you know it."

Belinda swallowed, her mouth dry. "Maybe I want to get burned," she replied breathlessly.

"Uncle Derek, Toby has to go to the bathroom, and so do I," Tasha called.

Derek jumped up from the blanket and Belinda expelled a tremulous sigh. "Okay, we'll call it a day and head inside."

"We have to potty bad," the little girl exclaimed, hopping on one leg, then the other.

Belinda stood. "You go ahead and take them. I'll gather up this stuff and follow right behind."

Derek hesitated only a moment, then he and the two kids took off hurriedly in the direction of the house.

As they disappeared from sight, Belinda expelled another deep sigh. It was probably a good thing Tasha had interrupted them. For a moment Derek's eyes had blazed with a heat that threatened to consume her.

He'd gotten her message, knew she wanted him. Now all she had to do was wait for him to figure out that she wanted him forever.

She bent and grabbed the edges of the blanket. Shaking off the leaves and grass, she thought back over her conversation with Janice.

It had been such a relief to tell somebody not only about the true circumstances of her marriage to Derek, but also about the tragedy of her baby's birth. That particular event had festered inside her for too long, and sharing it with Janice had felt good. She folded the blanket, then picked up the basket.

"Belinda."

She whirled around in surprise as Janice stepped out of the brush and into the clearing. "Janice. Oh, my gosh, I was just thinking about you. What are you doing here? Did you forget something when you left this morning?"

"Yes...I forgot something." She reached into her purse, an odd expression on her face.

Belinda froze in surprise as she withdrew a gun and leveled it at her. "Janice, what are you doing?"

Janice's lips curled upward in a smile, but her eyes radiated an emptiness that terrified Belinda. "I'm taking back what's mine."

"What are you talking about? I don't understand." With the barrel of the gun pointed at her, Belinda remained frozen, afraid to move a single muscle. "Janice, put the gun down and let's talk."

She shook her head, the gun not wavering. "I can't do that. You have to die. It's the only way he'll love me again."

Slowly, dreadfully, knowledge filtered into Belinda's brain. Janice had dated Derek right before Belinda and Derek had begun their relationship. "Oh, Janice," she breathed softly. "It was you all along? You broke into my house? Ran me off the road?" She remembered the bruise on Janice's shoulder, a bruise caused by the recoil of a shotgun butt. "You tried to shoot me?"

"You've been an exceedingly lucky victim. But your luck just ran out."

"But...what about Roger?" Belinda asked, frantic to keep her talking, to buy herself time...time for Derek to realize she hadn't followed them and something was wrong. "I thought you cared about him."

"Roger?" Janice barked an amused laugh. "Roger is nothing but a temporary amusement." Her eyes blazed with anger and madness. "Derek is the only man for me. He's always been the only one for me. But you ruined everything."

"You sent those notes to Derek?"

Janice nodded. "It was a test, and he failed. I figured if I sent those notes about you and he didn't return here, then he no longer cared. My plan was to go to California and resume our relationship." Her gaze narrowed and sheer malevolence radiated toward Belinda. "But he came running back here, running back to you. Always you. Always you." Her voice rose shrilly. "Now turn around. It will be easier if I shoot you from behind."

"Wait..." Time. Belinda needed time. Janice's hand holding the gun was steady, too steady for Belinda to take a chance rushing her. All she could hope was that she could keep Janice talking long enough for Derek to return.

"Please...I deserve some answers. Was it you who set fire to Derek's house?"

Janice's features paled. "That was a mistake. I lost control. I saw you and him together that night, making love in his room. I knew his parents were gone and figured you two planned to spend the night together." She gripped the gun so tightly her hand was white. "I was so angry my mind went red. I left and got some gasoline and rags, then I returned and sneaked into the house and set the fire. I didn't know you'd already left."

Tears filled Belinda's eyes. As she realized the love she'd felt for Derek had spawned such evil in Janice, her heart ached for them all.

"It was crazy," Janice continued. "I didn't want to hurt Derek, I just wanted you two to stop. I wanted to make you go away. I wanted you to die, but you didn't. And now you have him once again, but this time you will die and I'll get him back."

"Janice." Derek stepped out of the woods and into the clearing. Belinda nearly sagged to the ground in relief. "Give me the gun," he said, his voice smooth, his features carefully schooled to reveal nothing.

"No. Don't come any closer, Derek," she warned, her composure shattering at his appearance. "Damn. You weren't supposed to be here. You weren't supposed to know." Her hand trembled, but not enough to spoil her shot if she pulled the trigger. "I know you'll be upset for a while, but I'll make you forget her. I'll make you so happy you won't grieve for long."

"Janice, you need to give me the gun." Derek remained calm as he advanced a step toward her.

"Right now we can fix what's happened, but if you pull that trigger, we won't be able to fix things."

"Stop. Don't come any closer," Janice screamed as tears raced down her cheeks. "I don't want to hurt you, Derek, but I want her dead…dead."

"Uncle Derek." Tasha's childish voice cut through the air and diverted Janice's attention. With the agility of a mountain lion, Derek leapt toward her. The gun went off with a roar and Belinda screamed as splinters from the tree next to her hit the side of her face.

She sobbed as Derek and Janice scuffled on the ground, fighting for control of the weapon. As she saw Tasha and Toby, frozen with fear at the edge of the clearing, she rushed to them. "Run. Run back to the house," she commanded. They all screamed as the gun went off once again.

The kids took off running and Belinda turned back to the couple rolling on the ground. Frantically she searched for a limb or something she could use as a weapon to help Derek. Before she could find anything useful, Derek managed to gain control of the gun. He stood as Janice remained on the ground, sobbing in despair. "Go to the house and call the sheriff. Tell him where we're at, then stay there with the kids."

Belinda nodded. What she wanted to do was go to him, hold him close, assure herself he was fine. But now was not the time.

As she hurried back to the house, myriad emotions swept through her. Horror, as she thought of how close she'd come to being killed. Sadness, as she realized the depths of Janice's madness. And finally, relief that it was all over.

It was still difficult to believe that it had been Janice all along. Janice who'd extended a hand in friendship merely as a means to get closer for the kill.

Janice breaking into her house. Janice shooting a gun at her. She touched her neck. Janice's hands wrapped around her throat. So strong. The strength of madness, Belinda supposed.

And it had been Janice who had forced her off the road on the night of the Harvest Moon Dance. She'd been driving a car off her father's lot, and that's why Belinda hadn't recognized the car.

Still, nothing, no thought could be stronger than her utter relief. Over. All the threats, all the danger. She had her life back. Now all she had to do was find out if that life would include Derek, not just for a year, but forever.

DEREK KNEW that for the rest of his life, the madness, the twisted love in Janice's eyes would haunt him. He'd only had a handful of dates with her, had never been intimate with her at all. But somehow, in her mind, their relationship had expanded, become all-consuming...an obsession.

Dusk painted purple shadows amid the trees as he walked back to the house. Long after Junior had arrived and taken Janice away, Derek had sat beneath one of the trees, trying to get a handle on his rage.

Rage. It was what had driven Janice to start the fire that destroyed his life. And it was what flowed through him as he thought back on everything Janice had said to him while they'd waited for the sheriff to arrive. She'd begged, she'd pleaded, and finally she'd spewed Belinda's secret, all in an effort to cajole Derek into letting her go.

He paused as the house came into view. Staring at it, he tried to imagine Belinda inside. He was certain she'd be nearly beside herself, wondering what had happened after the sheriff arrived, why Derek hadn't immediately returned.

He hadn't returned because his rage had frightened him. His grief had nearly undone him. It had been the possibility that Janice had lied that finally drew him toward home. He had to know if Janice had lied, or if Belinda's betrayal, her hatred of him, ran deep enough for her to keep such a devastating secret.

She met him at the door, her eyes dark with worry. "What happened?" she asked as they went into the living room.

"She's been arrested and will be charged with attempted murder." He sank onto the sofa. "Where are the kids?"

"Asleep. Between the fresh air and the excitement, they were worn out. I decided an early bedtime would be in everyone's best interest." She sat next to him on the sofa. "It's just so hard to believe that it was Janice all along. She must have loved you desperately."

Derek frowned. "What she felt for me had nothing to do with love. Love isn't crazy. Love doesn't set fires." He looked at her, wanting desperately to believe Janice had lied. "And love doesn't keep secrets. Tell me about the baby, Belinda."

Her face blanched of all color. "She told you."

Any hope that Janice had lied disappeared, replaced by a choking anger that propelled him off the sofa. "I want you to tell me. Dammit, I want you to tell me what happened to my baby."

"Your baby?" Red stains of color returned to her cheeks as her eyes flashed with an anger of her own. "You negated any right you had to the baby when you wrote me that letter telling me it was over."

"No matter what happened between the two of us, I had a right to know that you were carrying my child." His heart felt as if it were made of crystal and she'd just fired a killing shot into the center of it. "Dammit, Belinda, I had a right to mourn for my son."

He drew a steadying breath, his eyes searching her face with incomprehension. "How could you lie next to me in bed and not tell me about him? How could you marry me, for any reason, and not tell me about the son I'd lost?"

"What difference does it all make now? It's done, it's over." Tears spilled from her eyes.

This was wrong, all wrong, Derek thought in some distant part of his mind. They should be grieving together, supporting each other in the loss of the baby. But she'd had two years to mourn and his grief was still too fresh to share.

She got up from the sofa and walked over to him, tears making her eyes shine like blue diamonds. "Derek, please..." She reached out to him and he knew she wanted what he'd just thought...to mourn with him. She wanted him to hold her, wanted them to grieve like other parents—together.

He couldn't do that. He was still too filled with anger, still too stunned by the unexpected information. He turned from her and strode to the front door. "I'm going out for a while. By the time I get home, have your things moved from the master suite back to the guest room. I think we need some space.''

He didn't wait for her answer. He walked out into the cold night, his leg ache just a mere irritation compared to the pain in his heart.

Chapter Fifteen

By the time Derek returned to the house, night had fallen and Belinda had not only moved her things from the master suite, but had also come to a painful decision.

She couldn't stay here. It was asking too much for her to remain in a marriage to a man she loved but who would never love her. It was too much to mother two loving children for a period of time, then walk away from their lives.

She'd been sitting in the living room when Derek had returned. He'd gone directly to the master bedroom and closed the door behind him. Belinda knew in closing her off from their bedroom, he'd conclusively shut her out of his life.

It was ironic that even in her defeat, Janice had managed to do what she'd set out to accomplish: she'd made certain that Derek and Belinda wouldn't share a future together. Derek would never forgive her for keeping the baby a secret, and he'd never love her like she longed to be loved.

Belinda knew Derek wouldn't penalize her sisters by withdrawing his financial support when she reneged on their agreement of a yearlong mock marriage. She'd do nothing toward obtaining a divorce until she was certain Derek had full, permanent custody of the children. But she couldn't live with him, couldn't share the days and nights with him and keep her sanity.

Before leaving she paused first in Tasha's doorway, then in Toby's, taking a last, lingering look at the children she'd grown to love. Her heart ached with the pain of leaving. But she couldn't stay. It hurt too much to love Derek and not be loved in return.

It was after ten o'clock when she walked quietly down the stairs, turned off the security alarm, and stepped out the front door.

A full moon peeked out from above wispy night clouds. She lingered on the porch, heart heavy, wishing things could be different, but knowing they never would be. She'd seen Derek's eyes when he'd turned away from her. They'd been filled with such betrayal, such pain. She couldn't remain where she wasn't wanted. And he didn't want her.

Stepping onto the dew-dampened grass, she whispered a soft goodbye. Eventually she'd make arrangements to get her clothes and personal items from Derek. There was nothing here she couldn't live without for a few days. Nothing except Derek, and that was no longer possible.

Her heart ached with each step that took her closer to the Connor ranch. Funny, how just in a space of days the family ranch no longer felt like home.

Home was Derek's house, with the children's laughter and Derek's arm around her. Home was breakfast in the morning with Derek's brown gaze warm on her, waking up with his body pressed close to hers.

The full moon cast eerie shadows on the landscape around her. She would never have considered this night journey had Janice not been caught. With Janice arrested and in jail, Belinda knew the danger to her was over.

Besides, Belinda had never been afraid of the dark, nor had she ever felt unsafe in the shadowed moonlight that night brought. It had been in the heart of night that she and Derek had often met to share a lovers' tryst. It had been in the darkness of night that they had pledged their love to one another. She would never be afraid of the dark, only the harsh reality of dawn.

She froze in her tracks as she heard a crackle of brush nearby. Perhaps an animal scurrying home to a snug burrow, she thought. Another snap of brush, then the slap of a foot against dried leaves. If it was an animal, it was an animal with big feet. "Hello?" she called tentatively. "Is somebody there?" She gasped as a figure stepped out from the brush.

"Belinda?"

She sighed in relief as she recognized Roger's voice. "Roger, you scared the life out of me," she exclaimed.

"Sorry." His teeth shone in the moonlight as he grinned and stepped closer to her. "You surprised me, too. What are you doing out here at this time of night?"

"Coming home. What about you?" She wondered if he'd heard the news about Janice, dreaded having to be the one to tell him if he hadn't heard.

His grin fell away. "I couldn't sleep." He swept his hat off his head, his blond hair gleaming silvery in the lunar light. "Belinda, I don't know what to say about Janice. Had I known…had I realized…"

Belinda placed a hand on his arm. "None of us could know. She's sick, and she hid that sickness well. I'm sorry, Roger. For you…and for me." She dropped her hand and leaned against a tree trunk, suspecting Roger needed to talk as much as she did. "It's still hard for me to believe that Janice hated me so much."

"Everyone was talking about it before bed," Roger replied. "I guess it's the kind of news that spreads like wildfire."

"I figured as much." Belinda was grateful that while Derek had been out she'd thought to call her sisters and explain the situation to them. She hadn't wanted them to hear about Janice through the grapevine. "She sure had me fooled." Belinda wrapped her arms around her shoulders to still a shiver. "I'm just glad it's over and I can get on with my life."

"Yeah, Janice was one of a kind, but she was incredibly stupid."

Belinda looked at him in surprise, wishing his face wasn't shadowed by the limbs of the trees. "What do you mean?" she asked.

Again she saw the white flash of Roger's teeth. "If she'd been smart, she'd have killed you and not been caught."

Belinda felt a ripple of unease at his words. She tensed as he took another step toward her. "Yes, Janice was dumb, but she wanted the same thing I did."

"And what's that?" Belinda asked, every nerve in

her body screaming warnings she didn't understand, couldn't comprehend.

"She wanted you dead." With a single, smooth movement, he pulled something from his pocket. A click sounded and the moon glinted off the blade of a wicked-looking knife. "Although this little moonlight meeting was unplanned, it provides a perfect opportunity for me to finish what Janice tried desperately to accomplish."

Belinda felt as if she'd been thrust into a nightmare. For a moment she couldn't move. Stunned inertia held her captive. "Why?" she finally managed to whisper.

"Janice told me you're the one. You're my half-sister, my father's daughter." His eyes glittered in the moonlight, as frightening as the knife he held in his hand. But he seemed to be in no hurry to use it; he acted with the confidence of a man who knew he had plenty of time to accomplish his goal.

"At first I wasn't sure which of the three of you it was. I figured I'd just make sure you all suffered tragic accidents."

"You pushed Colette off the butte," Belinda said in shock, remembering the night months ago that Colette had nearly plunged to her death.

"True. And I locked her in that cellar. And I also dropped a bale of hay on Abby, hoping it would break her neck." He laughed and shook his head with a rueful smile. "But you Connor girls are hard to kill."

"I still don't understand. Why would you want to kill us? What have we ever done to you?"

"You exist." The words exploded from him, sharp as gunfire. He drew a breath, as if to steady himself.

"It's nothing personal, Belinda. You see, the problem is, I hate my father. I hate him with every fiber of my being. Before he dies I want to be able to lean over and whisper in his ear that I killed the daughter he'd always wanted."

The inertia that had gripped Belinda shattered with his horrifying words. Acting with survival instincts alone, she pushed off from the tree trunk and ran.

Fear made her clumsy, awkward, and she tripped and fell to one knee. Sobbing, she pulled herself up and raced on. The moonlight that had aided her earlier was now an enemy, keeping her far too visible to Roger's pursuit. Thick brush and trees made running fast difficult and holes and ruts impeded her further.

She knew screaming would be a futile waste of energy. She was between the two ranches, too far away for anyone in either house to hear.

Within moments a stitch ached in her side and her breathing became labored. Still she ran, dodging between trees, careening through bushes.

She finally paused behind the trunk of a large oak tree, needing to get her bearings and catch her breath. Where was Roger? She clasped a hand over her mouth, trying to still the ragged breaths that tore at her lungs. She couldn't hear him.

Had she lost him? Was it possible he'd lost sight of her in the moonlight? Pressing her back against the tree as if she could disappear into the wood, she listened for any sound, any indication that he approached.

All the night creatures had fallen silent. The only sound she heard was the slight rustle of the leaves as the wind moved amid leaves above her head. Where was he? Should she run or should she remain here, frozen like a frightened rabbit?

Placing a hand over her pounding heart, she leaned to peek out from behind the tree. Moonlight bathed the immediate area. No sign of Roger.

Maybe I lost him, she thought. Hope surged within her, but she tamped it down, recognizing that she was far from being out of danger.

If she could just get to the Connor bunkhouse, Bulldog wouldn't let anyone harm her. Or to the house, where her brothers-in-law would keep her safe.

She screamed as Roger suddenly loomed in front of her, his teeth shining as he grinned in triumph. She turned to run, but cried out as he managed to snag her braid in a firm grasp. Pain exploded at the nape of her neck as she struggled to free herself.

"Don't fight it, Belinda," Roger exclaimed as he grappled to maintain his hold on her. "Make this easy on me and I'll see you die a quick death. Make it hard and I promise you'll suffer."

Belinda kicked out blindly behind her, jubilation surging through her as her foot connected solidly with his groin. His grip on her hair instantly loosened as he cursed and sank to his knees.

Once again she ran, terror sweeping through her as she heard his pursuit, the promises of what he'd do to her when he caught her. "I'm going to kill you, sweet little sister. I'm going to slice your throat." He raged. He laughed. He promised. And Belinda's blood ran cold.

She had no idea where she was, in what direction she ran, until she saw the dragon tree ahead. She didn't think it through. As she heard Roger closing on her, thought was no longer possible. When she reached the tree, without hesitation, she began to climb.

The tree was not an easy tree to scale. Years of familiarity, years of practice, gave Belinda knowledge of the secret knots and crevices, the nearly hidden footholds, that would allow somebody to ascend up to where the lowest branches were out of reach from anyone on the ground.

When she reached those branches, she paused to catch her breath. She peered down to the ground, her heart leaping into her throat as Roger circled the base of the tree.

He laughed, the sound sending shivers racing down Belinda's spine. "Looks like you've got yourself up a tree, little sister."

"You'll never get away with this, Roger," she replied, hoping—praying—he couldn't climb trees and that he suffered a severe case of fear of heights.

"I practically have gotten away with it," he returned. "I'll admit, there's been times I thought you Connor sisters had more than your share of guardian angels. But it appears yours has finally gone on vacation." Again he seemed to be in no hurry as he circled the tree where she had effectively cornered herself.

"Roger...this is crazy. You can't know for sure that I'm your sister and even if I am, what do you hope to possibly accomplish by killing me?"

"Your death will destroy him. I want that. I want to see his eyes when I tell him I killed you. I know you're the one. Janice made me see that you're the one."

"Janice wanted you to believe that," Belinda exclaimed in frustration. "She wanted me dead for her own purposes. You're playing right into her hands."

"Shut up. You should already be dead. I nearly had you on the night of your party."

Belinda gasped, remembering the feel of those strong hands around her throat. She'd been right all along, they had been male hands. Roger's hands.

"Roger, Janice used you." She tried to reason with him. "It's not too late to stop this."

"I don't want to hear any more. I'm tired of talking." He jumped in an attempt to grab the lowest branch, but it was out of his reach.

Belinda watched in horror as he gripped the knife between his teeth, then ran his hands along the trunk of the tree, seeking the holds that had aided her in her climb.

She heard his grunt of satisfaction, then he began to clamber after her. Belinda moved higher, refusing to speculate what would happen when she reached the top and there was no place else to go. When she'd gone about halfway up the tree, she paused again and looked below her.

She could just barely see the top of his head. His progress was slow...but each move he made brought him closer to her. Sooner or later he would reach her. There would be no place else to climb and he would be close enough to thrust the knife into her.

With a sob of despair, she moved higher. As her foot stepped into the juncture where two large branches met, she heard the odd sound of her boot hitting metal.

Still hanging on to the tree with one hand, she bent

and with her free hand touched the coolness of metal. Quickly, aware of Roger's steady climb toward her, she ran her fingers across the surface. It felt like a box. A metal strongbox tucked into a shallow cavity.

She didn't stop to consider how it had gotten there, didn't care what it might contain. To her, the box represented one thing. A weapon. Her fingers scrambled to loosen it from its hiding place. She gasped as it came away from the wood, and held it to her chest.

It was too unwieldy to swing like a bat, too heavy for anything but... She looked down to where Roger was visible through the branches that separated them.

As she stared down at him, he looked up. At some point during his climb he'd taken the knife out of his mouth and once again had it in his hand.

He saw her peering down at him and smiled, his eyes gleaming in evil anticipation. "Where are you going to go, sweet sister? You going to fly out of the top of the tree?" He laughed, the laughter ringing discordantly through the night.

He turned his attention back to his ascension, moving first hands, then feet to bring him closer...closer to her. A sudden, deep exhaustion crept through Belinda.

Too much. The events of the day, the emotional traumas had all been too much. All she wanted to do was curl up in the arms of the dragon tree and cry.

First Janice, who'd set a fire that destroyed any chance of happiness she and Derek would ever have. Now Roger, whose madness promised an end to her life. Anger usurped exhaustion. Rage surged inside her. How dare these people play with her fate? How dare they orchestrate her life like demented puppet-eers?

With a cry of outrage, she raised the strongbox above her, then dashed it down at Roger.

She heard the sickening thud as it connected. He grunted and lost his hold. With a helpless cry, he fell, his body crashing through limbs and branches before falling to the ground.

Staring to where he lay face-down, unmoving, Belinda wondered if it was a trick. Was he hurt, unconscious...or was he playing possum, waiting for her to climb down where she'd be an easy target?

She crouched in the cradle of the two limbs, unsure what to do. Minutes ticked by. Long, agonizing moments of indecision.

Even if he was unconscious, sooner or later he'd come to and when he did, he'd come after her again. She couldn't just wait for that to happen. Cautiously, she lowered herself, pausing at each level to look down at Roger once again.

"Belinda?" Derek's voice, like a beacon of light in the darkness, rang out in the distance.

"Over here, Derek," she screamed. "By the dragon tree."

He stepped out of the brush and into the clearing by the tree. In an instant his gaze took in the scene of Belinda in the tree and Roger unmoving on the ground. "Are you all right? What happened?" he asked as he squatted next to Roger's body.

"Is...is he dead?"

"No. He's out cold, but he's breathing. Belinda, what in the hell is going on?"

"He tried to kill me. Look around...he had a knife."

Derek found the knife near the base of the tree, and only when he had it in his possession did Belinda leave her perch.

She went directly into his arms, burrowing her face in the front of his shirt as she shivered uncontrollably with residual fear and overwhelming relief. As he held her close, she told him everything that had happened.

Roger moaned, signaling approaching consciousness, and Derek released Belinda and used his belt to tie Roger's hands behind his back.

"We'll take him home and call the sheriff." Derek smiled at her and touched her cheek with the back of his hand. "We seem to be calling Junior a lot lately."

"I hope after tonight I never have reason to call him again," Belinda replied fervently. She longed to lean against Derek once again, press her face into the warmth of his touch, but she knew better than to give in to her need. Him holding her, his hand against her cheek, meant nothing personal, was the expression of sympathy for the ordeal she'd just been through.

As Derek pulled Roger to his feet, she bent and picked up the metal strongbox that had saved her life. Together they walked toward Derek's house. Roger moaned, his eyes darting wildly as if seeking escape, but Derek held him firmly.

When they got back to the house, Derek tied Roger to a kitchen chair, called Junior, then motioned Belinda to the sofa. "Go on, sit and relax. I'd say you've had one hell of a day."

She sank onto the sofa and closed her eyes, willing

away the tears that formed. The exhaustion that had plagued her before returned and with it an uncontrollable need to cry.

She wanted to cry for all that Janice had destroyed when she'd set that fire years before. She needed to cry for the two children upstairs, children who had lost their parents and believed Belinda would be their mommy on earth.

"Are you all right?"

She opened her eyes to see Derek watching her. She nodded and flashed him a forced smile, then closed her eyes once again. No, she wasn't all right. She loved Derek with all her heart and soul, but he didn't return her feelings. He didn't love her enough to want a forever with her. She wiped at an errant tear. No, she would never be all right again.

Chapter Sixteen

The eastern horizon was just showing signs of dawn when Junior took Roger away in handcuffs. It had been a night of revelation as Roger had told them his responsibility in many of the near-tragic accidents that had befallen the ranch.

He'd bragged about how close he'd come on so many occasions to hurting one of the women, railed at the injustice of his ultimate defeat.

It had been frightening to listen to him spew his hatred of his father, more frightening that a man filled with hate had teamed up with a woman filled with passion to make a matched pair of potential killers.

Derek and Belinda watched the patrol car pull away, the headlights fading into the predawn illumination. "Now it's time for us to talk," Derek said when the car had disappeared from sight.

"What's left to talk about?" Belinda wrapped her arms around her shoulders and gazed out into the distance. She was tired. So very tired. She had nothing left with which to fight her love for him.

"Belinda...please."

She turned and looked at him. Although his face

was drawn with lines of tiredness, he would always be the man of her dreams, the prince of her fantasies.

"Come on, come inside with me," he suggested.

With a resigned sigh, she nodded, unsure whether the chill that suffused her was because of the cool outside air or the ache in her heart. "Where are you going?" she asked as he started up the stairs.

"We'll talk in the bedroom, where we can close the door and the kids won't wake up."

Belinda hesitated. "Derek, if you want to rehash the past, then forget it. We can't change anything and I'm too tired to fight."

"I don't want to fight, either. But we need to talk, Belinda. You owe me that much."

He was right. She knew now she should have never kept the baby a secret. She should have told him, no matter what their personal circumstances were. She followed him to the master suite, where he closed the door, then turned to face her. "Why did you leave here tonight? Where were you going?"

"Home." She sat on the edge of the bed, averting her gaze from him.

"Your home is here."

She shook her head. "No, Derek. I was fooling myself when I agreed to this temporary marriage thing. I'm sorry. I know we made an agreement, but it's one I can no longer abide by." Her voice dropped to a whisper and she looked at him once again. "I can't do it, Derek. I can't pretend anymore."

His eyes darkened and his jaw clenched. "I didn't realize pretending to be my wife would be such an onerous task. I didn't realize pretending to love me would be so disagreeable."

Belinda laughed, surprised when it came out as a strangled sob. She was too tired for games, and it was too late for pride. "Oh, Derek, are you truly so obtuse? It isn't hard pretending to love you. What's impossible for me is pretending not to love you."

He stood still, frozen as his eyes searched her face. "What do you mean?" He didn't blink, didn't move a muscle.

"What do you think I mean?" she replied in resignation. She got up from the bed and went to stand at the window, where the sun sent pale gold shafts of light across the eastern sky. Dawn. The promise of a new day, but no promise of happiness for her.

"I love you, Derek." The words eased out of her on a sigh. She couldn't face him, didn't want to see his expression as she bared her heart. "I loved you three years ago and I think I'll love you for the rest of my life." She heard his swift intake of breath, but didn't turn around. "I'm sorry, Derek. I know you were honest when you told me you didn't want emotional entanglements. But I'm hopelessly entangled."

Her voice dropped to a whisper once again. "I can't live the next year with you, wake up every morning with your arms around me, then walk away when the adoption is finalized. I...I just can't do it."

It was only then that she turned to face him. He still stared at her, but the expression on his face was not what she'd expected. His eyes gleamed with a nakedness, no shutters to hide the expression there. Desire. Tenderness. And, yes, love. It shone from his eyes with intensity.

"You love me." Astonished joy winged through her as she recognized the expression on his face. She walked over to where he stood and placed her hands on either side of his face. "You do love me, don't you?" she whispered.

His eyes blackened as he twisted away from her caress and took a step backward. "It doesn't matter what I feel for you. I told you from the very beginning that I didn't want this. Dammit, this wasn't supposed to happen."

"I don't understand." Belinda searched his face beseechingly. "I love you and I believe you love me. What's wrong with that? Why do you want to turn your back on that love?"

His hands clenched and unclenched and a muscle ticked an irregular rhythm in his jaw. "I'm not the man I was three years ago, Belinda."

"Perhaps not, but you're still the man I love, the man I want to spend the rest of my life with." Each word she spoke seemed to bring him more pain. "Three years ago I made a vow to you. You remember?" She moved closer to him, so close she could feel his breath on her face, feel the heat that emanated from his body.

"Three years ago I told you I'd love you until the moon fell out of the sky and melted on Main Street in Cheyenne. As far as I know, that particular phenomena hasn't occurred." Again she pressed her hands against his cheeks. "I love you, Derek, and nothing is ever going to change that."

He seemed to crumble into himself. He closed his eyes and drew in a tremulous breath. When he looked at her again, his eyes were filled with tears. "Belinda...sweet Belinda." He covered her hands with his, and once again Belinda's heart filled with joy as his gaze lavished her with love.

"Don't you understand?" His voice was filled with anguish. "It's too late for us. Three years too late."

The joy Belinda had felt was short-lived as she heard the resigned regret in his voice. She pulled her hands away from him. "It's because of the baby, isn't it? You can't forgive me." Her heart ached with her own regret. "I know I should have told you, Derek, but I was so scared and confused. I didn't think it mattered and I thought my grief would keep me safe from loving you. But it didn't."

"Shh." He placed a fingertip against her mouth. "Like you, I'll forever carry the grief in my heart for our child, but this isn't about that."

Belinda backed away from him, feeling the first stir of anger. "Then tell me what it's about."

Once again dark shutters fell across his eyes, obscuring any emotion from her view. "Just take my word for it. There's no future for the two of us. Don't worry, I'll live up to my agreement with your sisters even if you decide to go back there to live." Pain flashed once again in his eyes. "Just leave it alone, Belinda."

"I'm not going to just leave it alone." Tears of frustration blurred her vision. "I've had a crazy woman try to kill me because I love you. I left here because I love you and put myself in the path of another homicidal maniac. No more secrets, Derek. No more secrets between us. If you love me, but can't be with me, then tell me why."

For a long moment he looked at her, his expression

one of infinite dread. "Fine," he snapped. "You want to know, then I won't tell you, I'll show you."

His hands trembled as he unfastened his belt. "What are you doing?" she asked when he began to unsnap his jeans.

He didn't answer. Instead he pulled down his jeans and stepped out of them, leaving him clad in a pair of briefs and exposing the scars that puckered and mottled his thigh. "This is why...because I'm no longer the golden boy with the beautiful body you loved."

"Oh, Derek." Belinda ached for him as she realized this had been his secret, his shame.

"By the time I woke up on the night of the fire, the roof was in flames. A burning timber fell on my leg. It seemed like it took forever for me to get it off and by then the damage had been done." His voice was devoid of tone and he didn't look at her, but just past her.

"At first they talked about taking off the leg. The bone was shattered and most of my flesh and muscle had been burned away. But they finally decided to reconstruct it. They did a good job. Unfortunately their cosmetic ability was rather lacking."

He looked at her with dead, unemotional eyes. "I watched my mother turn away from me time and time again with revulsion in her eyes and I swore to myself I'd never see that expression again from another woman." He swallowed hard. "I knew I wouldn't be able to bear it if I saw it from you."

He reached for his jeans, but Belinda was quicker. She grabbed them and threw them across the room. "You remember when I cut my knee in the shed and we ran inside to have your mother help bandage it?'' He didn't look at her, nor acknowledge her words. "There was a lot of blood, but the cut wasn't very deep. Still, your mom went pale as a ghost and ran for the bathroom. She couldn't handle the sight of blood or wounds.''

"This is a little more serious than a skinned knee,'' he replied bitterly.

"Yes, it is.'' Belinda stepped toward him. "It's terrible and tragic, but any disgust I feel is for the woman who set the fire that did that to you.'' She placed her hand against the scarred wound, felt his swift intake of breath. "I love you, Derek. Scars and all. And the only way you'll disgust me is if you turn your back on our love.''

A strangled sob caught in his chest and for a breathless moment he remained still and unyielding. Then, with a sob, he pulled her tight against him, his arms wrapping around her as if he'd never let her go. "Oh, Belinda. I do love you,'' he moaned into her hair. "I've been so afraid...so very afraid that you'd see my leg and not want me. I'd rather you hate me than pity me.''

He kissed her, his mouth moving with fire and ice from her lips, down her jaw. "I told myself I was just coming back here because you were in danger. I tried to convince myself that the only way to keep you safe was to marry you. I was only kidding myself, looking for any excuse to be with you.''

Belinda looked up into his eyes, the soft brown eyes she loved. "And I tried to tell myself the only reason I was marrying you was to help out my sisters.

But deep inside I just wanted another chance to love you."

He framed her face with his hands. "When I think of you in that tree, trying to fight off Roger—" He broke off and hugged her again.

"Derek—the strongbox." Belinda suddenly remembered what had saved her life. "We need to open it, see what's inside."

"Later." His eyes blazed with a fire that stole her breath away. "First we're going to plan our wedding."

She laughed. "But we're already married."

"Oh, yeah, that's right." He smiled, the slow grin that caused heat to unfurl inside her. "Then first I'm going to make love to my wife."

He scooped her up into his arms and carried her to the bed. As they passed the window Belinda saw the sky bright with the light of dawn. The promise of a new day. She looked at her husband and saw the dawn light reflected in his eyes. The promise of love.

IT WAS SOMETIME LATER when Belinda, Derek and the two kids walked to the Connor ranch with the metal strongbox in hand. Belinda had a hunch, and she didn't want to open the box without her sisters being present.

The adults had gathered around the kitchen table and the kids had been sent to Cody's room to play when a knock sounded at the back door.

Abby opened the door to Junior Blanchard. "Morning, Abby." He peered around her and saw Belinda and Derek at the table. "Ah, thought I'd find the two of you here. I had a long talk with Senator Whinnert's aide this morning and thought you might want to hear about it."

"Come on in and I'll pour you a cup of coffee," Abby said.

Junior swept off his hat and pulled a chair up to the table. He looked at the three sisters, a smile deepening the lines around his eyes. "I'll tell you one thing, you Connor girls sure know how to keep things jumping around here."

"It has been a wild couple of months," Colette said with a smile.

"Yeah, well if you think this kind of wild stuff is gonna continue, let me know. I'll hire another dozen men just to keep up with you all," Junior teased, then sobered. "Unfortunately, not all the news I bring with me this morning is good."

"Don't tell me Roger escaped," Belinda exclaimed, and reached for Derek's hand.

"No, no, nothing like that. Roger Whinnert isn't going to see the light of day for a very long time. He and Janice will be prosecuted to the fullest extent of the law." He paused a moment to sip his coffee, then leaned back in his chair and eyed them all solemnly. "Senator Whinnert passed away last night. Apparently he went peacefully, in his sleep."

Belinda looked at her sisters. If Roger had been telling the truth, then one of them had lost their biological father. Belinda searched her heart for grief, but could find none. There was only an impersonal sadness for the passing of a stranger.

"At least he'll never know Roger's wicked plans," she said softly.

"And that's a blessing," Junior agreed, then continued. "According to the aide I spoke to, Roger had been in trouble most of his life. From what I've learned, Roger was a disturbed little boy who grew into a disturbed young man. The senator kept cleaning up his messes and giving him more chances. This is one final mess the senator won't be cleaning up."

Junior drained his coffee mug and stood. "Well, just wanted to stop by and tell you what I knew." He smiled at them fondly. "Your mother and father would have been proud of the three of you. You've come through rough times, but you're all survivors."

"Of course, we're Connor women," Abby replied proudly. The three sisters smiled at each other.

"I guess we should open the box," Belinda said when Junior had left. The metal strongbox sat in the middle of the table, like the guest of honor at a party.

"You think the adoption papers are inside?" Colette asked as she leaned into her husband's side.

"I do," Belinda replied. "We haven't been able to find them anyplace else." She pulled the box over in front of her and stroked the lid thoughtfully. "You know how Mama loved that tree. Somehow it makes sense that she'd put the papers there."

Abby smiled, her eyes soft with memories as she turned to her husband. "Mama taught us how to climb that tree when we could barely walk. Daddy used to tease her about being part monkey, but she'd just laugh and tell him the dragon tree was like part of her soul."

"And she made it a part of us," Belinda said. With fingers that trembled, she unfastened the clasp. "You know, it doesn't matter to me," she said before opening the box. "It doesn't matter to me who has adoption papers in here." She looked at Colette, then at Abby, her heart expanding with love. "You are my sisters, and no piece of paper is ever going to change that."

"I feel the same way," Colette said vehemently.

"Me, too," Abby added.

They smiled, and Belinda knew they were all remembering a night long ago, a night when a vow was made under the boughs of the dragon tree. That night, in their youth, the thought of one of them being adopted had been terrifying. Now, with the wisdom of adults, they knew no papers would ever taint what they felt for one another.

Belinda opened the box. A manila envelope marked "adoption papers" was on top. She lifted it out, surprised to find another envelope similarly marked beneath it. And a third beneath that. She looked at her sisters, whose expressions of shock mirrored hers.

"It's all of us," she said in wonder. "Three sets of papers for three baby girls."

"I'll be damned," Derek said softly.

"So, what do we do now?" Colette asked.

"I guess we open them," Abby replied.

Belinda held one of the envelopes, stared at it thoughtfully, then placed it back in the strongbox. "I don't need to open it." She smiled at her sisters. "I know who I am, who my family is. If I ever feel a need to know more, I can always open them later."

Colette put hers back in the box. "I feel the same way."

"At least from this day on we'll know where the

papers are,'' Abby said as she added her envelope in with the other two.

They all watched silently as Belinda refastened the clasp, locking away the papers Roger had so desperately wanted found.

''And now, I'd better get busy,'' Abby said as she stood. ''I've got a ranch to run here.''

''And you promised me a trip into town for some supplies,'' Colette reminded Hank.

Derek and Belinda stood. ''And we've got things to do at home,'' Belinda replied. Home. Her heart thrilled at the thought. Home with Derek. Home with the children. She smiled at Derek, her husband...her heart. ''Let's get our kids and go home.''

The answering smile he gave her filled her with happiness. Belinda knew her dawn had finally come, a dawn filled with the promise of forever with the man she loved.

Epilogue

"Pass me some more of the potato salad, please," Colette said. "What about you, Derek...ready for something to eat?"

Derek shook his head and touched his stomach. "I can't. I just can't right now."

The entire family was gathered on a blanket, enjoying a picnic after the long winter months of snow and cold. The May air simmered with the fragrance of blooming flowers and sun-warmed earth.

"I think maybe I'm coming down with a touch of the flu or something," Derek said as he stretched out on one corner of the blanket.

"You've been fighting off that flu bug ever since Belinda started having morning sickness," Colette said with a sly smile.

"Who would have thought a macho man like Derek would suffer morning sickness," Abby teased.

"It's not funny," Derek replied. "And it's not morning sickness. I just have a queasy stomach right now."

Belinda smiled at the conversation and rubbed her burgeoning stomach. "I have a feeling my husband's stomach problems will be better in about four months when I deliver this little bundle of joy.''

As the conversation turned to ranching business, Belinda thought back over the past months. She'd never known this kind of happiness before. Each day brought new joys, a deeper passion and a renewed commitment in her marriage.

Toby and Tasha were thriving and thrilled at the prospect of a new little brother or sister. She caressed her stomach again. When she'd discovered herself pregnant, Derek had insisted she go to the best doctor in town, who assured her that she should have no problems delivering a normal, healthy baby.

Although there would always be a space in her heart for the child she'd lost, the new life growing inside her helped ease that pain.

''You okay?'' Derek asked, his brows furrowed in worry as he watched her rub her tummy.

''I'm fine,'' she assured him.

He scooted over beside her and placed his hand on her belly. ''You are better than fine. You are the most beautiful woman in the world. You're my life.'' His eyes flamed with fires of love and desire.

Belinda's heart expanded and as always when he looked at her that way, she felt a delightful breathlessness. ''My, Mr. Walker, you do know how to sweet talk a girl.''

''Okay, you two. Knock it off.'' Abby laughed. ''Derek, are you sure you don't want something to eat before I call the kids over. You know they'll demolish what's left.''

''Go ahead and feed them. I'm fine.''

''I wonder what they're doing out there,'' Colette

said as she stood to look out toward the dragon tree where the children were all gathered at the base.

"Probably weaving fantasies of dragons and kings, and warriors and princesses," Abby replied.

"And if they're very lucky, their fantasies will come true. Cody and Toby will find lovely princesses to love for all their lives, and Brook and Tasha will find handsome princes to make them happy for the rest of their lives." Belinda smiled at her husband. "Just like we did," she said softly. "Forever," she spoke in a whisper only Derek could hear.

"Until the moon falls down in the middle of Main Street and melts all over the city of Cheyenne," he replied. She smiled. "Forever," he echoed and in his eyes, that's exactly what she saw.

"WE'RE COUSINS, and that means we're family. And family always loves and protects each other," Cody said to the others.

"Protect…" Toby echoed with a grin. Brook babbled in toddler fashion from Tasha's lap.

"But we're adopted," Tasha said.

"That don't matter," Cody scoffed in seven-year-old fashion. He spit through his teeth in the cowboy way just like Bulldog had taught him. He couldn't do it in front of his mother. She scolded him.

"We're cousins and that's for sure," he continued. "We're gonna make a pact. We help each other and if trouble comes, we fight it together. Okay?"

"'Kay," Toby replied.

"All right," Tasha agreed.

"Mamamamama," Brook added, clapping her hands together and drooling down her chin.

"All for one and one for all." Cody stuck his hand out and put Toby's on top. "Come on, Tasha. Put your hand on ours, then Brook's."

She nodded and put her hands on the boys' hands. Brook pat-a-caked her hand on the very top.

"Cousins forever," Cody said. "Family for always."

Tasha and Toby repeated his words, and a soft breeze stirred through the dragon tree and for a moment warm sunshine played on their features.

"Okay, now let's go eat!"

As the kids ran toward their parents and the awaiting lunch, the dragon tree danced in the breeze, then seemed to reach its limbs up to the cloudless blue sky.

HE SAID

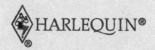

SHE SAID

Explore the mystery of male/female communication in this extraordinary new book from two of your favorite Harlequin authors.

Jasmine Cresswell and Margaret St. George bring you the exciting story of two romantic adversaries—each from their own point of view!

DEV'S STORY. CATHY'S STORY.
As he sees it. As she sees it.
Both sides of the story!

The heat is definitely on, and these two can't stay out of the kitchen!

Don't miss **HE SAID, SHE SAID.**
Available in July wherever Harlequin books are sold.

HARLEQUIN®

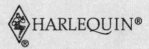

And the Winner Is...
You!

...when you pick up these great titles
from our new promotion at your
favorite retail outlet this June!

Diana Palmer
The Case of the Mesmerizing Boss

Betty Neels
The Convenient Wife

Annette Broadrick
Irresistible

Emma Darcy
A Wedding to Remember

Rachel Lee
Lost Warriors

Marie Ferrarella
Father Goose

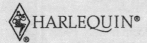 

Imagine that you've traveled far away, to a place of heady danger and luxurious romance nestled high in the Colorado Rocky Mountains. The bellhop has left your bags, and you're about to unpack in a room you'll share with a sexy man....

Welcome to the

Honeymoon Hideaway

This summer, reader favorite Sheryl Lynn brings you this exciting duet in June and July. Don't miss her upcoming romantic mysteries:

#424 THE CASE OF THE VANISHED GROOM
#425 THE CASE OF THE BAD LUCK FIANCÉ

Harlequin Intrigue invites you to make your vacation escape to the HONEYMOON HIDEAWAY!

HARLEQUIN®

I N T R I G U E®

HMH

You are cordially invited to a

HOMETOWN REUNION

September 1996—August 1997

Bad boys, cowboys, babies. Feuding families,
arson, mistaken identity, a mom on the run…
Where can you find romance and adventure?
Tyler, Wisconsin, that's where!

So join us in this not-so-sleepy little town and
experience the love, the laughter and the
tears of those who call it home.

WELCOME TO A
HOMETOWN REUNION

Tyler's vet, Roger Phelps, has had a crush on
Gracie Lawson for fourteen years. Now she's
back in town and he still wants her madly. But
Gracie couldn't possibly carry on romantically with
the boy who used to pack her groceries. Even if
the man he turned out to be is gorgeous, gentle,
funny and passionate.… What would people say?
Don't miss *Puppy Love* by Ginger Chambers,
tenth in a series you won't want to end.…

June 1997
at your favorite retail outlet.

HARLEQUIN®